## MURDER INTERRED WITH
## HIS BONES

Apart from themselves the site was deserted. The only sound was the purr of the metal detector as Horace guided it over a partly infilled trench. He started as it abruptly emitted a loud high-pitched note.

"Something under here all right," Jim exclaimed. "Gimme the trowel."

Bending down he worked energetically, throwing out scoops of rubble. About eighteen inches down he struck a hard object. Almost immediately they both noticed the unpleasant smell. For Horace it instantly resuscitated wartime experiences long and mercifully forgotten. Before he could speak, Jim had succeeded in levering up a sheet of corrugated iron. With a strangled gasp he let it fall back again.

"God Almighty," Horace said hoarsely. "It's a police job, this."

BANTAM BOOKS offers the finest in classic and modern English murder mysteries. Ask your bookseller for the books you have missed.

## Agatha Christie

DEATH ON THE NILE
A HOLIDAY FOR MURDER
THE MYSTERIOUS AFFAIR
  AT STYLES
POIROT INVESTIGATES
POSTERN OF FATE
THE SECRET ADVERSARY
THE SEVEN DIALS MYSTERY
SLEEPING MURDER

## Carter Dickson

DEATH IN FIVE BOXES
THE SKELETON IN THE
  CLOCK
THE WHITE PRIORY
  MURDERS

## Catherine Aird

HENRIETTA WHO?
HIS BURIAL TOO
A LATE PHOENIX
A MOST CONTAGIOUS GAME
PASSING STRANGE
THE RELIGIOUS BODY
SLIGHT MOURNING
SOME DIE ELOQUENT
THE STATELY HOME
  MURDER

## Patricia Wentworth

THE FINGERPRINT
THE IVORY DAGGER
THE LISTENING EYE
MISS SILVER COMES TO
  STAY
POISON IN THE PEN
SHE CAME BACK
THROUGH THE WALL

## Elizabeth Lemarchand

BURIED IN THE PAST
DEATH ON DOOMSDAY

## Margaret Erskine

THE FAMILY AT
  TAMMERTON
NO. 9 BELMONT SQUARE
THE WOMAN AT
  BELGUARDO

## Margaret Yorke

CAST FOR DEATH
DEAD IN THE MORNING
GRAVE MATTERS

## Ruth Rendell

A DEMON IN MY VIEW
THE FALLEN CURTAIN
A SLEEPING LIFE

## June Thomson

ALIBI IN TIME
CASE CLOSED
THE LONG REVENGE

## E. X. Ferrars

ALIVE AND DEAD
EXPERIMENT WITH DEATH
FROG IN THE THROAT
LAST WILL AND TESTAMENT
MURDERS ANONYMOUS

# Buried in the Past

Elizabeth Lemarchand

BANTAM BOOKS
TORONTO · NEW YORK · LONDON · SYDNEY

All characters and events portrayed in this
story are fictitious

*This low-priced Bantam Book
has been completely reset in a type face
designed for easy reading, and was printed
from new plates. It contains the complete
text of the original hard-cover edition.*
NOT ONE WORD HAS BEEN OMITTED.

BURIED IN THE PAST

*A Bantam Book / published by arrangement with
Walker and Company*

*PRINTING HISTORY*

*First published in the United States of America
1975 by Walker Publishing Company, Inc.*

*Bantam edition / October 1982*

ISBN 0-553-22830-7

PRINTED IN THE UNITED STATES OF AMERICA

O    0   ᵒ   8   7   6   5   4   3   2   1

To
S.M.G.R. of Lady Margaret Hall, Oxford
and
J.A.Y. of the University of Exeter
whose erudition sparked off
this book.

# Chief Characters

**The Ancient Borough of Corbury**

| | |
|---|---|
| MARK PLOWMAN | Owner of Plowman's Pottery |
| MONICA PLOWMAN | His wife |
| BELINDA PLOWMAN | His daughter, a student at the Warhampton College of Art |
| GERALD STANTON | Solicitor and Town Clerk |
| SHIRLEY STANTON | His wife, sister of Mark Plowman |
| SIR MILES LEWARNE OF EDGEHILL COURT | |
| HORACE RUDD | Employee of Value Foods Limited |

**The County Town of Allchester**

| | |
|---|---|
| ADRIAN BERESFORD | Assistant Archivist |

**The Conurbation of Warhampton**

| | |
|---|---|
| BERNARD LISTER, M.A., B. LITT., F.R. HIST. S. | Lecturer in Medieval History at the University, cousin to Mark Plowman and Shirley Stanton |
| JAMES HALTON, D.SC. | Ornithologist, neighbour to Bernard Lister |

**The Law**

Superintendent Thomas of the Corbury Constabulary
Detective-Inspector Worrall of the Warhampton CID
Detective-Superintendent Pollard and Detective-Inspector Toye of New Scotland Yard

# Part One

# Chapter 1

The Editor
The Corbury Courier                                    6 November

Dear Sir,

As the Bible says, a thousand years are but as yesterday. With the Millenary coming on fast Corbury hearts beat with the same pride as their forefathers' did, when good King Edgar made us a free borough and gave us a site for St. Gundryth's Church where it stands to this day.

I take up my pen, sir, to urge on the Council, as you keep doing in the paper, to celebrate our Millenary in a manner befitting past, present and future.

Long live the Ancient Borough of Corbury!

Your obedient servant,
Horace J. Rudd

6 Beaconsfield Road
Corbury.

The *Corbury Courier* came out on Fridays. While he was shaving, Horace Rudd heard the front gate squeak, and a muffled thud on the mat. He ran downstairs, his face soaped, and scooped up the newspapers. In the kitchen he threw aside the *Express*, and spread out the *Courier* on the unoccupied end of the table. With hands that fumbled slightly he turned to the section headed What Our Readers Think. Incredulous delight swept over him as he saw his letter under the sub-heading "Roll on, Millenary Year." He read through it rapidly, then more slowly, awed by this incontrovertible evidence that he was one of the paper's Thinking Readers.

"Winnie!" he shouted in the direction of the back kitchen. "They've put it in!"

A roundabout figure in bedroom slippers appeared in the doorway, borne in on a waft of frying bacon.

"Going to the shop like you are?" his wife enquired. "Give us a look."

Horace Rudd showed her the *Courier*, jabbing at his letter with a finger. He watched her lips move as she read it.

"They'll offer you a job on the paper, I shouldn't wonder," she commented, concealing her pride under irony. "All the same maybe you'd better finish out the week down at the shop before you asks for your cards. Bacon's just gone into the pan, if you want any breakfast."

He gave her a resounding slap on the bottom with the *Courier*, and ran up the stairs two steps at a time.

Half an hour later he left the house walking jauntily, a dapper little figure with bright dark eyes and strands of carefully arranged thinning hair. His workplace, Value Foods Limited, a supermarket in the High Street, was a bare ten minutes' walk. Corbury was still small and compact, though expanding. The old town—the parish church and the select residential area—was on the crest of the downland scarp. Later development had crept down a gently-sloping spur into the vale below. Value Foods was conveniently situated between the two worlds. This morning Horace Rudd could not get to work soon enough, exhilarated at the prospect of a still further enhanced status in the eyes of staff and customers. Life was unexpectedly branching out for him: earlier in the year he had been mentioned in the *Courier* as a volunteer helper in the excavation of a Roman villa near the church.

When Sir Miles LeWarne of Edgehill Court came down to breakfast, he found the folded *Times* and *Courier* by his place. An elderly widower, wealth and local status enabled him to maintain a fair standard of gracious living. He read the chief news items on the front page of *The Times* over the excellent coffee and crisp toast provided by Maggie Marsh, his housekeeper, and then carried off both papers to his study. He had plenty of leisure for them now. He was an active eighty-one, and sometimes the days seemed long. He had come off the Bench under the new age-limit rule, and had reluctantly resigned from his many committees in the course of the past decade, deciding that it was better to remove oneself than to dodder on, keeping out a younger man. The LeWarnes, who had been at Edgehill Court for over three centuries, were a Corbury tradition, however, and his many invitations to public functions still kept him in touch.

Sir Miles settled himself in his favourite chair drawn into a patch of sunshine, got his after-breakfast pipe going nicely, and opened the *Courier*. Because of a lifetime's association with the town, almost every item in it was meaningful to him. Eventually he arrived at Horace Rudd's letter, and a smile lit up his tired old face with its big nose and mouth, and blue eyes under bushy white eyebrows. He remembered Horace as an out-at-elbows errand boy when old Fairbrother owned the shop, and a damn sight better shop it was in those days, too. He found it heartwarming that the older generation, at any rate, had pride in their town. . . .

At eleven o'clock Maggie Marsh brought in his Bovril and biscuits. She urged a scarf, as well as an overcoat, for the turn in the garden which he took before lunch on fine mornings. It was sharp, she told him, in spite of the sunshine. Anxious care of him showed in her honest, frog-like face under a frizzled fringe. Sir Miles suppressed his irritation at being fussed over, and promised to comply.

"Everything under control for Mr. and Mrs. Roger tomorrow?" he asked, to turn the conversation.

"Everything, sir. Mrs. Hayes is doing out the bedroom and dressing room now, and Finch is sending up a nice shoulder of lamb first thing, with a brace of pheasants for Sunday lunch, like you said."

"Splendid," he replied, and began to sip the Bovril—a hint to her to withdraw.

When she had gone his eyes wandered to the photographs of his wife, who had died ten years earlier, and of his son and only child, shot down while piloting a bomber over Germany in the last war. As so often, he tried to picture the family circle, augmented by grandchildren, which might have surrounded him now. It troubled him that this imaginative exercise seemed to become more difficult as the years slipped by. He turned for reassurance to the wedding photographs of Roger LeWarne, his great-nephew and heir. A dear boy, Roger, and he'd married a fine girl. At any rate there was a LeWarne to carry on the title, and keep up the old place. Time they were making a start on a family, though. . . .

Presently, overcoated and with a white scarf to protect his throat, Sir Miles stepped out on to the terrace. It was a still morning of late autumn, with a pale blue sky and fragile sunlight. Walking with a stick and an old man's caution, he descended to the rose garden on the lower terrace. There were still a few belated blooms. He took out a pocket knife and cut a bud from a persistent Frensham for a buttonhole, re-creating the fine upstanding chap that he had been, not all that long ago.

Going slowly up the steps to the first terrace again, he walked to its far end, and stood looking across the town. Between Edgehill Court and Corbury the scarp curved inwards, forming a shallow bay. As he gazed, Sir Miles picked out buildings he knew well: St. Gundryth's Church with its fine perpendicular tower, the scheduled Georgian houses of Edge Crescent, the waterfall of bricks and mortar tumbling down the scarp to the regimented modern layout in the vale. Straight as a ruled line, the road which the Roman legionaries had made came out of the distance, cutting across the flat ground to the town, ascending the spur as Corbury High Street, and vanishing past the church.

What an eye for the lie of the land those fellows had, Sir Miles thought, as he turned towards his front door.

Stanton & Mundy, Corbury solicitors, took in the *Courier*, its contents often being relevant to their clients' affairs. Gerald Stanton, senior partner and Town Clerk, sat studying the advertisements of forthcoming property sales over his elevenses. He then skimmed through the rest of the paper. The words "Roll on, Millenary Year" caught his eye, and he read Horace Rudd's letter with a grin. Had it ever occurred to the chap that the befitting celebrations he was clamouring for would have to be paid for by somebody? Gerald Stanton congratulated himself on having persuaded the Borough Council to open a Millenary Fund, in the hope of being able to avoid levying a special rate. It had got off to a flying start with a blockbuster of a thousand pounds from old Miles LeWarne, too. And there was the chance that another of his inspirations might pay off: the invitation to the Mayor of Corbury, U.S.A., to attend the celebrations.

The firm's office was at the top of High Street. Gerald Stanton, a tall, dark man in his early forties, got up to deposit his coffee tray on a side table and stood looking out of the window. A continuous stream of traffic was entering and leaving the town by the long, straight road across the vale: a satisfactory sight. Stanton was a member of a small local syndicate, recently formed to acquire and modernize a dreary little commercial hotel with an eye to the increasing tourist industry of the area. Subconsciously, thoughts of finance directed his attention to the buildings of Plowman's Pottery, a family business owned by his brother-in-law. As he frowned, the buzzer on his desk sounded.

"Mr. Catwick's here, Mr. Stanton," his secretary informed him.

"Show him in," he replied, his mind instantly switching to the pros and cons of Mr. Catwick's buying the freehold of his house.

Mr. Catwick was followed by another client who was facing a charge of driving without due care and attention, and it was just on one o'clock when Gerald Stanton left the office to go home to lunch. His home was in the status-conferring Edge Crescent, whose beautifully-proportioned houses in mellow brick Sir Miles LeWarne had admired earlier that morning. Number One had been a wedding present to the young couple from his father-in-law, the late James Plowman. Shirley Plowman had been fully aware that she was marrying up, out of trade into the professional classes. Over the years she had applied her intelligence and inherited business acumen to harmonizing the interior of her new home with its elegant exterior. The result was admirable, and today, as almost always, Gerald reacted with pleasure as he came in. He sensed at once, however, that something had ruffled Shirley.

"Anything come unstuck?" he enquired presently over lamb cutlets. "You look a bit hipped."

Shirley Stanton, a few years younger than her husband, was a well turned out pale woman, with straw-coloured hair swept back into a bun. Fine, but rather challenging blue-grey eyes and a slightly square jaw gave her face the emphasis which its colouring lacked. At this moment there were faint red patches on her cheekbones.

"Sorry it's so obvious," she said. "I always feel you're entitled to a peaceful lunch hour. It's Mark, of course. I looked in at the Pottery this morning. The year's profits are going to be down by at least eight per cent."

Gerald raised his eyebrows.

"What did Mark have to say about it—if anything?"

"He started off by blaming everything and everybody else, and ended up by losing his temper and shouting at me. Of course, to be fair, one's got to admit that it's been a difficult year. A late cold spring always means a reduced demand for the horticultural lines, and it was a poorish August—fewer people around, and less to spend because of strikes. Wages and fuel and whatever, all up. I admit all that. It's the way he just sits down under it, instead of looking ahead and trying to develop new lines and find ways of cutting costs, that maddens me. For instance, I just can't get him to see that tourist demand for the better stuff is on the increase. He's taking the usual line that it would be unsound to get a bank loan for a second electric kiln if sales have fallen, and anyway skilled labour's short."

Gerald helped himself to cheese and biscuits.

"I suppose you made your usual offer?"

"Certainly I did. In fact, I improved on it. I said I'd advance the money for the kiln at half the Bank's interest, with repayment over the next three years, provided that I came in over all major policy decisions. He simply blew up, and said either he'd run the Pottery himself, or sell it up for what he could get. There's nothing to stop him, you know."

"It's not the slightest use my having another go at talking to him, I suppose?"

Shirley shook her head decidedly.

"None whatever. He'd only dig in."

"What I shall never be able to understand is why your old man didn't leave you a share in the business, instead of just a share of the profits. He must have realized that you've got about ten times Mark's grip."

"He'd never have done that. The Pottery has always come down from father to eldest son. In some ways Father and Mark have a lot in common. You know—'as it was in the beginning' etc. But of course profits were easier to come by in Father's day, so he made out nicely all the same."

"On a more cheerful note," Gerald said, "we've heard *sub rosa* that full planning permission has come through for the Royal Oak."

"That's something to be thankful for, anyway."

They began to discuss the scheme for the modernization of the hotel.

As well as the Pottery, Mark Plowman had inherited his father's house in Edge Crescent, and lived there with his wife Monica, and only child Belinda, a few doors from the Stantons. Monica Plowman, now in her late thirties, was a kind-hearted unambitious woman, inclined to be lazy, and engrossed by her home and family and a small circle of personal friends. Neither she nor her husband had seen any reason to refurnish their new home when they moved in fifteen years earlier, and its rooms presented an oddly dated appearance. Apart from modernization of the kitchen premises, and the contemporary décor of Belinda's bed-sitter, executed by herself, little had changed since Mark's childhood.

Belinda was now eighteen, artistically gifted, and at present taking a course in industrial design at the Warhampton College of Art. Her psychological make-up combined her aunt's ability and purpose with her mother's capacity for sympathy, and in consequence a fair measure of communication between herself and her parents had been maintained as she grew up. Gathering from a rather woolly letter from her mother that things were going badly at the Pottery, she had unexpectedly come home for the weekend, announcing to her fellow students that she felt like a spot of lushness, and was in need of a cash handout.

After a large tea in front of a blazing log fire she sprawled in an armchair, in what was still called the drawing room. Against its cream walls and chintzes she struck an incongruous note in scruffy blue jeans and a purple sweater, one leg dangling over an arm of the chair. Her fair hair was worn long and straight, and tumbled in confusion over her shoulders. It framed a face broad at the cheekbones, with a good brow and the Plowman blue-grey eyes.

"Aunt Shirley is a bitch," she commented, as her mother's account of the morning's encounter between Mark and Shirley at the Pottery came to an end. "But all the same, Mummy, I do think Pop could get up and go a bit more, you know. This kiln thing: you've simply got to take chances if you want to turn over lolly these days."

"Everything to do with running a business is dreadfully difficult now," Monica replied, having firmly grasped at least this one economic fact, even if unable to elucidate it. "Everything is so uncertain, you see. Your father feels he can't possibly launch out unless he can see his way ahead. He seems very worried, I'm afraid."

Belinda's gaze wandered round the room, and rested on family photographs in silver frames. She began to speculate about life in the days when people took it for granted that things would go on in the same way for ever.

"Mummy, I've seen Bernard Lister," she said, through an association of ideas.

Monica Plowman looked up quickly from her sewing.

"You mean your father's cousin?" she asked in an astonished tone.

"Who else? Bernard Lister, M.A., B.Litt., F.R.Hist.S., Lecturer in Medieval History in the University of Warhampton. I happened to see on a poster that he was giving a public lecture, and thought I'd go along to have a look at him."

"I've never met him," her mother replied, suppressing obvious curiosity. "He'd broken with the family before your father and I knew each other."

"He's small and pale—looks clever and unathletic. D'you know," Belinda went on meditatively, "I don't blame him a bit for walking out. He must have had a perfectly bloody time with Aunt Shirley and Pop when they were all kids. He'd have been a hopeless misfit in the Plowman set-up."

"I think he behaved disgracefully," Monica said with unusual vigour. "Your grandparents took him in when he was a friendless orphan without a penny, brought him up with their own children and gave him a good education. Then simply to write and say he'd never set foot in the house again as soon as he came into money when he was at Oxford . . ."

"Well, anyway, he's done his thing. Been an academic success, I mean. It was a jolly good lecture. He's had things published, too."

Belinda picked up the *Corbury Courier* which she had let fall to the floor, and began to glance through it idly.

"This Millenary racket seems to be catching on," she remarked presently. "Here's a gorgeous letter about hearts beating in pride, and whatever. They ought to invite Blister, as his loving cousins called him, to come down and talk about Corbury's past glories."

"For heaven's sake, Belinda, don't suggest anything of the sort to your father. Better not to mention that you've seen Bernard, in fact."

"O.K., O.K., Mummy. I know Blister's a dirty word to Pop and Aunt Shirley. Listen! That's Pop coming in, isn't it?"

She scrambled to her feet and ran out into the hall.

"Hiya!" she called.

"Lindy!" Mark Plowman turned from shutting the front

door with an exclamation of pleasure. "I'd no idea you were coming home."

He enveloped her in a bear's hug, and then held her at arm's length, looking at her anxiously.

"There's nothing wrong, is there?"

"I'm not preggers, and I haven't been sent down for any other reason, if that's what you're thinking," she told him with a broad grin.

"Really, you girls of today," Monica expostulated from the drawing room door. "Mark, you're very late. You must be tired out. I'll get the drinks tray and we can have a nice cosy time round the fire before supper."

"Come on Pop, relax," Belinda adjured him. "Forget about the Pottery for once."

Later, as they sat over their drinks, it struck her with a sharp pang that her father was beginning to look old. His hair, which had always been so fair and thick, was becoming grizzled, and creeping back from his temples. Even when she made him laugh at some lighthearted anecdote, the lines about his eyes and those running down from the corners of his mouth were still there. One day he'll die, she thought, struggling with an embarrassing lump in her throat, and I'll miss him so dreadfully. . . .

"Pop," she said on impulse when her mother had gone to the kitchen, "why not sell the Pottery? Move into a smaller house and live on much less in peace and quiet? Mummy wouldn't mind—in fact, she'd like it. What's the point of being bothered to death by the blasted place? We only have one life, so what?"

Mark Plowman gave her a quick look, and his expression became guarded.

"It isn't as simple as all that, I'm afraid, Lindy," he said abruptly.

As he spoke, the telephone rang and he got up swiftly to answer it. She stared after him, vaguely disquieted. The next moment he called from the hall.

"One of your boy friends, from the sound of it."

Forgetting family problems, she ran eagerly to take the call.

Bernard Lister had the *Corbury Courier* posted to him regularly, and it normally arrived by the first post on Saturday mornings. If asked why he took in the local newspaper of a town which he had no intention of ever revisiting, he would have said wryly that its petty parochialism, epitomized in the *Courier*, heightened his satisfaction at having escaped from the place. He had no idea that in reading about Corbury he was indulging a masochistic desire to recapture his desperately unhappy childhood and adolescence there.

Jack Lister, his father, had been a chauffeur employed by the parents of Mrs. James Plowman, mother of Mark and Shirley. Her younger sister, Muriel, had eloped with him in the nineteen twenties, and subsequently married him. Her outraged family had broken off all contact with her, and so were unaware of her death in giving birth to Bernard. Jack Lister had been brought up in an orphanage with a brother who had emigrated, and lost touch. Devoid of relations, he did the best he could for his little son with the help of good-hearted neighbours, but when he himself was carried off by a virus pneumonia, there was nothing for it but Local Authority care for Bernard, then aged six. Enquiries were set on foot by the Authority, and ultimately his mother's family was traced. With considerable reluctance Bernard was taken into the James Plowmans' nursery, to be brought up with Mark and Shirley, respectively a year older and a year younger than himself.

By no stretch of imagination could he have been described as an attractive child. He was pale, undersized and awkward, with a thick working-class accent and a number of unrefined habits. Sensitive, he was paralysed by the vast size and incomprehensible demands of his new home in Edge Crescent, and instantly aware of his unacceptability to the household. His aunt and uncle were kind, but he tried their patience to the utmost. Mark and Shirley, big tall children, confident and good at games, despised and resented him, resorting to physical bullying when they felt safe from observation. Later on, this gave place to mimicry of his speech, which never quite lost the traces of his early life, and the use of the hated nickname Blister, derived from the unfortunate juxtaposition of his initial and surname.

All three children were sent in due course to Corbury Grammar School. Here it rapidly transpired that Bernard was exceptionally intelligent, a fact which his aunt and uncle could not help finding unpalatable, especially in relation to Mark's very average ability. As a result he got little praise and encouragement at home, and was condemned as a swot and a dud at games in school. He withdrew increasingly into the world of books and ideas, a lonely boy, with no close friends and a deep sense of injustice. Then, at seventeen, he startled Corbury by winning major scholarships to both Oxford and Cambridge. The school was an Edward VI foundation with endowments for promising pupils, and under pressure from the Headmaster and Governors, the James Plowmans agreed to Bernard's going up to Oxford and deferring a career which would make him financially independent of them.

The miracle happened in his second year. His father's brother died in Australia, leaving an estate of £50,000 to his brother Jack or his heirs. In the event Bernard inherited. His reactions were few and decisive. On emerging from the office of the London solicitors with his identity established, he found his way to St. James's Park, and sat there for some hours, oblivious of his surroundings. Then, abruptly surfacing, he asked a policeman the way to the nearest post office. Here he bought a letter-card, and wrote a concise statement of his changed circumstances to his aunt and uncle, adding that they would not see him or hear from him again. Having posted the letter-card, he returned to Oxford with the intention of taking a First—which he achieved—and of devoting himself to an academic career.

Now, twenty years later, on this fine Saturday morning in November, he sat over a leisurely breakfast in his comfortable bachelor flat at Warhampton, his second ambition also fulfilled. His surroundings reflected the way of life that he had chosen, partly in accordance with his personal tastes, and partly as a defence against a society which, he felt, had largely rejected him. Except in the sphere of his work he was by choice a recluse, greatly preferring his own company to that of others, and apprehensive of women and their suspected predatory designs. He remained basically insecure, and capable of violent emotional reaction to threats, real or imagined, to his security.

On reaching the toast and marmalade stage he ripped off the wrapper of the previous day's issue of the *Courier*, and began to scan its pages with a critical eye. His eye was caught by Sir Miles LeWarne's name in a list of guests at a public dinner, and one of his rare happy memories of Corbury came back to him. On being awarded his scholarship he had been summoned alone to Edgehill Court, greeted with kindly interest, and presented with a cheque for ten pounds with which to buy books. Afterwards he came to realize that the study where he had been received had impressed him even more than the dignified donor, and the room in which he now sat had been modelled on it: the big knee-hole desk, the deep comfortable masculine armchairs, the bookshelves which lined the walls. . . .

As he perused further items Bernard Lister's habitual contempt for Corbury and its citizens returned in force. He was almost completely lacking in humour, and Horace Rudd's letter merely evoked a disgusted exclamation. Bogus tripe, he thought, and began to compose an acid reply dealing with the lack of reliable evidence of King Edgar's alleged dealings with the town in the tenth century. He could refer to the preposterous legend of St. Gundryth, an unverifiable personage said to have miraculously restored the King's favourite boarhound to life after it had been fatally gored by a tusker on a royal hunting expedition. Admittedly the parish church was dedicated to her, but obviously she should be relegated to the Vatican's recent list of fictitious saints.

Bernard absently buttered another slice of toast while debating various telling openings for his letter. Suddenly an even more promising idea occurred to him. Recently a series of charters claimed by another borough of vaunted antiquity had been found beyond any reasonable doubt to be forgeries. Suppose he could establish that Corbury's charters were in the same category? There was a whole series of them, he remembered. . . . Of course Corbury people would be incapable of appreciating historical evidence, but with the so-called Millenary coming up, the facts could be leaked to the Press, and the whole affair made to look ridiculous.

# Chapter 2

Oblivious of Bernard Lister's valuation and malicious intent, Corbury went about its business in the cheerful bustling atmosphere of a fine Saturday morning.

Soon after ten o'clock a fanfare on a car horn brought Belinda Plowman running out of the house. She was immediately driven off at speed in a sports car, by a young man whose apparel contrived to suggest both the Space Age and the Italian Renaissance.

Monica Plowman watched the departure from a window with a little sigh: her own upbringing had been wholly conventional. As a young mother she had often indulged in pleasant fantasies of a really big white wedding in St. Gundryth's for Belinda, with a reception to follow in a marquee in the garden. Rather less distinct, but equally enjoyable, had been pictures of herself surrounded in due course by charming well-behaved grandchildren. But up to now it had been patently impossible to cast any of Belinda's numerous boy friends for the role of bridegroom in morning dress, or as responsible young father. She sighed again, and turned away from the window to address herself to her programme for the morning. As she was fortunate enough to have a daily woman who worked on Saturdays, she was virtually free, and soon went out, officially to finish her shopping for the weekend, but mainly to meet a group of equally leisured friends for coffee.

The householders of Edge Crescent kept their cars in the former mews at the back, which were separated by a lane from the gardens behind the houses. This branched off from the road and ran down at the side of Number One, the Stantons' home, before turning right and giving access to all the garages. Lost in unco-ordinated thoughts about Belinda, the Pottery, and her prospective purchases, Monica walked straight in front of Gerald Stanton's car as it emerged from the lane. He braked sharply, concealing irritation with difficulty. Monica, who found both Gerald and Shirley intimidating, gave him a nervous smile, and stood dithering until he combined a sign to her to go on with a sketchy salute. He then backed the car to his front door. Shirley came out, shutting and locking the door after her, smart in country casuals for a lunch engagement with friends some two hours' drive from Corbury. They overtook Monica Plowman at the top of High Street, who gave a hesitant wave. Gerald mentioned his earlier encounter.

"She's hopeless," Shirley commented. "Look, she's actually wearing a hat! If only Mark had married the right sort of woman."

Plowman's Pottery worked a five-day week. Solitary in his office, Mark found its big echoing spaces depressing. As he stared at the papers on his desk, it seemed as though the silence was stealthily moving in on him, making it impossible to concentrate and arrive at the right decisions. He realized as clearly as his sister the need for expansion of the business. What she did not know was the extent of his borrowings from the Bank over the past few years, and the polite but inflexible refusal of the Manager to allow him any further latitude, either over the Pottery account or his personal one. If he accepted her offer of a loan how could the firm's financial position be kept from her? The prospect of her reaction was intolerable. . . . On the other hand suppose the Treasury, or whoever it was, started making Banks call in their money? Mark Plowman frowned heavily as his thoughts moved in an all too familiar circle.

At Edgehill Court Sir Miles LeWarne wandered around, unobtrusively checking up on the preparations for the young people's visit. Normally he used the study as his sitting room, but for the next two days the Court's beautiful drawing room opening on to the terrace would be in use. He went in to make sure that there was a good log fire to supplement the central heating, and sniffed the pleasant blend of wood smoke and chrysanthemums. Great pots of these had been brought in from the greenhouses, splendid blooms, white, gold and glowing bronze. He must remember to congratulate old Bryce, his gardener, on Monday and see that Celia took a couple of pots back to the London flat.

Too intent on the hours immediately ahead to let the room

evoke memories, he went back to the study and tried to
settle down to *The Times*. Only twelve o'clock: another half-
hour at least before he would hear the pandemonium of the
arrival with that yappy little dachshund. Still, it was a sport-
ing little fellow, and you couldn't keep a proper dog in a
flat. . . . The room was warm, and anticipation had wakened
him at an early hour. His head began to nod. . . .

He came to with a start, agitated to see the hands of the
travelling clock on the mantelpiece registering twenty minutes to one. He listened, and was relieved to find the silence
unbroken. They should be turning up at any moment now,
though. With lunch billed for a quarter past one there would
hardly be time for a drink first, unless they arrived soon.
Feeling the sudden irritation of the old at a threatened dis-
ruption of a plan, he got to his feet and went out into the hall,
where he caught an appetizing whiff of roasting meat. Faint
sounds of activity came from the kitchen region but otherwise
all was quiet. Suppressing an impulse to go and confer with
Maggie Marsh, Sir Miles returned to the study and sat bolt
upright watching the clock. At a quarter to one he could
restrain himself no longer and went to the kitchen.

"What on earth can be holding them up?" he demanded
testily. "The meal won't be fit to eat. We'll have to cut out
drinks, that's all."

"Why, they've been later than this before now, sir," Maggie
soothed. "It's the Saturday traffic, even at this time of year.
This fine weather'll be bringing out the cars. Don't you worry
about the lunch, sir. Nothing hurts in the simmering oven."

Partly reassured he once more returned to the study, and
watched the slow progress of the clock hands towards the
hour. A puncture, he thought, and quicker to change the
wheel than to hunt about for a telephone. If they'd had a real
breakdown, though, that was going to hold them up for some
time: well, they'd manage to ring somehow, surely? Involuntarily he glanced round at the telephone on his desk.

The minute hand began to drop from the vertical. Abruptly
the fear lurking on the threshold of consciousness insisted on
recognition. The old man's mouth went dry as he faced the
possibility of an accident. The minute-by-minute passage of
time ceased to matter. He sat frozen, reminding himself that
there were degrees of accident.

Suddenly the front door bell rang, a monstrous irrelevance
which angered him. Who the bloody hell was coming pester-

ing at a time like this? He listened to Maggie Marsh's quick steps in the hall. Then he heard voices, one of them a man's. Exasperation at the length of the conversation brought him to his feet. Why in God's name didn't she send the fellow packing?

Incredibly she was bringing somebody to see him. . . .

As he turned towards the door it opened, and Superintendent Thomas of the Corbury Constabulary walked into the room unannounced. Startled, Sir Miles stared at him uncomprehendingly. Then he saw the compassion in his face. . . .

During the afternoon the news of the Roger LeWarnes' fatal road crash spread rapidly over the Corbury grapevine. Shortly before four o'clock Monica Plowman was rung up by a friend whose brother had heard of the disaster at first hand from Superintendent Thomas himself. Dismay and pity for Sir Miles filled her mind to the exclusion of everything else. She hurried out into the garden to find her husband.

In an attempt to escape temporarily from his worries Mark Plowman had changed into an ancient sweater and a pair of dilapidated trousers, and was engaged in the autumn clearance of his herbaceous borders. A bonfire crackled conversationally in a corner, and as Monica crossed the lawn he was heading towards it with a heaped wheelbarrow. Catching sight of her he halted, with a look of irritated enquiry.

"Oh, Mark," she said, with a catch in her voice, "the most dreadful thing has happened." She swallowed as he stared at her. "Roger and Celia LeWarne. They've both been killed. In their car, coming down for the weekend."

Her husband abruptly released the handles of his wheelbarrow.

"My God, how absolutely appalling," he said slowly. "Was it near here?"

"I don't know. Jean Cooper's just rung me. She said another car had skidded into them: she didn't know where."

He frowned anxiously as a host of queries began to flood into his mind.

"I wonder if Shirley and Gerald have heard?" he said. "Somebody ought to go along to the Court. Uncle Miles may want phone calls put through, and so on. I don't know if Maggie's equal to that sort of thing."

Sir Miles, a lifelong friend of James Plowman, had been an uncle by courtesy to his children.

"I think Shirley and Gerald are out," Monica told him. "I saw them going off this morning in the car."

"Hell! I think I'll ring them on chance, though."

Abandoning the wheelbarrow in the middle of the lawn, Mark went quickly into the house, flung himself down by the telephone, and dialled the Stantons' number. He got the ringing tone which continued uninterruptedly.

"Obviously not back yet," he said at last, putting down the receiver with a clatter. He sat on, registering indecision, his hand absently drumming on the table.

"Don't you think you'd better go over to the Court yourself?" Monica ventured.

She got an irascible glance from his aggressively blue eyes, brighter and hotter than was usual in a Plowman.

"No, I don't," he replied categorically. "I'm damned if I'll have Shirley and her precious husband accusing me of sucking up to Uncle Miles. Be your age, darling," he went on impatiently. "The baronetcy becomes extinct—there's no male heir now, as we all know. But what about the property and the money? Uncle Miles is pretty well-heeled, isn't he? Don't forget that Shirley's his goddaughter, and Gerald his solicitor, now that old Harrison's dead."

Monica gave a small gasp.

"I hadn't thought of that."

"You wouldn't. I bet it'll be the immediate Stanton reaction, though."

But although easy-going, Monica Plowman could be persistent where her sense of right and wrong was involved.

"But Mark, suppose Uncle Miles really needs help? Just think—"

The sound of an approaching car brought her husband to his feet, and sent him to the window.

"They're back," he said. "Shirley's just getting out. I'll ring at once. Gratifying to be a beat ahead of her for once."

As he anticipated, his sister's horrified reception of the news was tinged with annoyance at getting it from himself. This expressed itself in a sharp enquiry about the source of his information. She rang off quickly, and within ten minutes Gerald Stanton drove along the Crescent in the direction of Edgehill Court.

Neither of the Plowmans noticed his return in the surprisingly short space of half an hour. In his absence Shirley had made herself some tea, and was sitting in her elegant drawing room drinking it. As he appeared she looked at him without speaking, her eyebrows raised interrogatively.

"No go," Gerald told her. "He's given orders that he'll only see the police or Doctor Lang. I tried to get past Maggie, but short of brute force it couldn't be done."

He subsided into a chair.

"I've always said that woman was too big for her boots," Shirley observed as she filled his cup.

"I agree. All the same, the poor old boy may feel he just can't face anybody who's personally involved with him. He must be completely shattered: his entire blueprint for the future centred on Roger, and he belongs to the stiff upper lip generation. All I could do was to tell Maggie to let him know I'd been over, and would come at any moment if he wanted me."

Gerald accepted the cup of tea, and helped himself to a slice of cake. Shirley leant back in her chair and considered.

"Don't let's pretend we aren't wondering where we may go from here," she said, after a pause. "Suppose I write a note, and go over in the car and drop it in?"

He looked at her speculatively.

"Just bung it into the letterbox, you mean? Yes, I think that would be the right touch. Don't knock up Maggie. One doesn't want to appear obvious."

### DEATHS

LEWARNE, Roger Miles and Celia Jane, as the result of a motor accident ON SATURDAY, 20 November. Cremation private. No letters, please.

While the notice in *The Times* was brief, the following week's issue of the *Corbury Courier* gave the disaster full coverage, including the inquest proceedings, which were adjourned to enable the police to make a full enquiry into the cause of the accident.

Sir Miles had insisted on being present at both the inquest and the cremation, and also at the short service of committal of the ashes in Corbury churchyard, next to his wife's grave. None of his many local friends were invited to be present, and after Celia LeWarne's parents and near relatives had left Corbury, he reverted to the seclusion of the days immediately following the disaster. It was nearly the end of the following week before Gerald Stanton was summoned to Edgehill Court.

As he drove out to it after supper, he admitted to a degree of inward excitement. As Sir Miles's solicitor he knew well that Roger LeWarne's death left the old baronet without a single known family connection. Shirley, his god-daughter, was already down for a useful legacy in the existing will, and there were no other godchildren whose ownership of the Court could be considered seriously on social grounds. So, if not Shirley, then who?

Gerald turned in at the drive gates, and drew up at the front door. He paused for a moment for a look at the perfect Regency exterior of the house, then went up the steps, bracing himself for a vitally important interview.

Maggie Marsh, a muted version of her normal self, ushered him into the study. He walked across the room with out-stretched hand, genuinely moved by Sir Miles's stricken, but controlled, appearance.

"Uncle Miles," he said, "I'm no good at putting these things into words, but you've hardly been out of our thoughts since this ghastly thing happened. And I know this is true of a good many people in Corbury."

"Thank you, my boy." Sir Miles indicated a chair drawn up on the opposite side of the hearth. "Sit down. Smoke, if you want to. Yes, I've sensed a lot of sympathy and goodwill," he went on, taking up Gerald's remark, "and this brings me to what I want to discuss with you. You've handled my affairs very well since Harrison's death, young though you are, and I've complete confidence that you'll wind up my estate com-petently when I've gone. It won't be long now."

"Don't say that, Uncle Miles," Gerald protested. "We—"

The old man cut him off, raising his hand.

"What have I got to live for now, my boy? All my plans and hopes for those two living here at the Court and raising a family have come to nothing, and the LeWarnes are at the end of their long road. All that remains is for me to dispose of my assets in a manner in keeping with our traditions. I have been giving a lot of thought to this matter during the past fortnight."

He paused. Gerald Stanton's trained ear detected an imper-sonal note which was not encouraging.

"Obviously," Sir Miles resumed, "I must make a fresh will, and to put my mind at rest I want you to draft it for me as quickly as possible. Briefly, this is to be the gist of it. I propose to increase most of the legacies to individuals and

charities in my existing will, but the legatees remain the
same, so that presents no difficulty. Roger, as you know, was
my residuary legatee, inheriting this place and its contents,
and the rest of my money. It's this aspect of the situation
that's been on my mind, pretty well day and night, and I
want to get it settled. You'll be glad to know that I've come to
a decision that satisfies me."

Gerald Stanton made an acquiescent murmur, and extracted
a writing pad from his brief case. He sat waiting, by now
convinced that some of Sir Miles's favourite good causes were
going to get the residuary estate.

"LeWarnes have lived here for a long time," Sir Miles
went on, after another pause, "and I like to think that over
the years we've been of service to the people of Corbury and
round about. Well, I want something of this service to go on
when there are none of us left. I've decided to leave the town
Edgehill Court, as it stands, and an adequate sum for its
future maintenance."

Completely taken by surprise, and bitterly disappointed by
the sweeping character of the bequest, Gerald Stanton was
for the moment bereft of speech. Then, glancing up, he met
the tired eyes, and recognized the irritation in them even
before Sir Miles spoke.

"Well, what's the matter? Don't you think it's a good plan
in the light of Roger's death and of what I've just been saying
to you? There can't be any legal obstacle, surely? As Town
Clerk and a qualified solicitor you ought to know."

"As far as I can see, none whatever, Uncle Miles," Gerald
told him, taking a firm grip on himself. "Of course, bequests
of this type need thinking out in detail. For instance, you
may wish to place restrictions on the use of the property.
Then there's the question of the right of alienation at some
future date. Trustees—"

Sir Miles broke in impatiently.

"What I want is for the place to be secured to the people of
Corbury in perpetuity, as far as this is legally possible. The
house is scheduled for preservation, so you chaps on the
Council can't pull it down, or start messing it about either, so
that should ensure its suitable use. You could move the
museum up here. With these Roman remains being exca-
vated it could do with more space. A lot of interesting stuff
may come to light. Chamber music concerts in the drawing
room. Conferences. That sort of thing. And if the money I'm

leaving for maintenance is competently invested, there should be ample funds for keeping the grounds in decent shape, as well as the house. I like to think of people enjoying them-selves up here with their children. Their children," he repeat-ed, half to himself.

Gerald Stanton, who had been making rapid notes, looked up to meet a keen glance.

"I hope I've made myself clear, my boy? It's up to you to sort out the details, and get it all into legal jargon. Now, about the increased legacies."

Sir Miles took up a sheet of writing paper, and began to read from it. Gerald heard that, as one of the executors, he had been left a thousand pounds, and that the original legacy of two thousand pounds to Shirley had been raised to five. His murmur of appreciation was brushed aside. A token bequest of five hundred pounds to Mark Plowman as the son of an old friend was to be a thousand. The legacies to the National Trust, and other organisations concerned with pres-ervation and the welfare of children were substantially increased.

"Well, that's it," Sir Miles concluded. "Have you got it all down? Right." He dropped the paper into the fire. "How long is it going to take you to draw up the will? I realize I'm not your only client, of course."

Gerald Stanton achieved what he hoped was a warm smile.

"You're in rather a special category, though, Uncle Miles. I think I could bring along a draft by the end of next week, if that would do?"

"Good. Just let me have a ring when you're coming. And, by the way, not a word of this must get out. There'd be too many chaps with an eye to future commercial possibilities. I'm not for a moment suggesting you're personally indiscreet yourself, as you know perfectly well, but what about your office staff?"

"That needn't worry you at all. I shall keep the whole matter in my own hands. I do quite a lot of work at home in the evenings, you know. Shirley's one of the rare women who understand about professional discretion. She never asks ques-tions. Incidentally she's away at the moment, at an exhibition got up by one of her societies, so I'll have plenty of time."

"Good. As I said, I'll be thankful to get all this settled. Shirley ought to have been trained for a profession herself—

she's got the brains for it. James Plowman was a fool to leave
Mark the sole control of the Pottery. I hear it's doing badly."

"Only too true, I'm afraid," Gerald told him, gathering up
his notes and preparing to leave.

He drove himself home with an overwhelming sense of
anticlimax. So that was that. The pipe dream had been really
exhilarating while it lasted. To own the status-symbol of
Edgehill Court, with ample funds to live up to it. . . .
Shirley, reticent by nature, had said little directly about her
hopes, but he knew her well enough to realize how sharp her
disappointment would be. He must get it across to her indi-
rectly that her godfather had had other ideas. Ideas that were
going to involve the hell of a lot of bother when the old boy
died, he reflected gloomily in his capacity of Town Clerk. It
was easy to foresee the endless argument and rows that the
bequest would generate. Uncle Miles was dead right about
not letting anything leak out now. People would be jockeying
for position at once. Not that there was any harm in unobtrusively looking around oneself. . . . If the present museum
were put up for sale, anyone owning the small shops next to
it would be sitting pretty. The site would be worth quite a bit
with Corbury expanding at its present rate. . . .

After Gerald Stanton had left, Sir Miles sat on for a time,
thinking in a desultory fashion, and drawing some comfort
from his conviction that he had made the best possible decision in the matter of his estate. Presently, aware that nothing
would induce the faithful Maggie Marsh to retire for the
night until she had heard him go up to his bedroom, he
levered himself up out of his chair, and put a fireguard in
front of the smouldering logs in the grate.

He had been sleeping so badly since Roger and Celia were
killed, sitting up in bed half the night making notes of his
ideas for his new will. Now that Gerald had got his instructions, perhaps he would be able to read himself to sleep once
again.

He stood for a few moments trying to recapture an infi-
nitely remote time in another world, when he had been
reading *Framley Parsonage* as his bedside book, and looking
forward to the young people coming down at the weekend.
With a sigh, he started on the journey upstairs.

Rather to his surprise he did have a better night, and
during the following week a half-unconscious adjustment to
the changed circumstances of his life began. A few old friends

were allowed to come and see him. He walked in the garden again, and began to glance through *The Times*. At mid-week Gerald Stanton rang to report good progress in drafting the new will, and made an appointment for Saturday.

He came after tea, and over drinks in front of the study fire they went through the will, clause by clause. Sir Miles declared himself completely satisfied with the terms of his bequest to Corbury.

"Well, I can't spot any holes in it, my boy," he said, "and if you feel it's watertight that's good enough for me. I suppose I can't sign the thing right away?"

"It would be a bit difficult to rustle up witnesses at this hour on a Saturday night, Uncle Miles. Bryce might be in his cottage, but he and Maggie aren't eligible, you see, being beneficiaries. Suppose I run over on Monday morning with a couple of clerks from the office?"

"All right. The sooner it's done with the better."

"Anyway, I'd like to leave the carbon copy with you over the weekend," Gerald went on, "just in case you change your mind about anything."

"That I certainly shan't do," Sir Miles replied vigorously. "Like that chap Pilate, what I have written I have written. Put the damn thing in the bottom left-hand drawer of the desk, will you, if you want to leave it here? Thanks," he added, as Gerald complied. "Help yourself to another drink. When's Shirley coming back?"

"On Monday afternoon, thank goodness. I'm sick of eating out, and the house is beginning to look tatty, in spite of our daily woman's efforts. . . . I don't know if you'd care for Shirley to look in next week, Uncle Miles?"

"Yes, yes. Let her come along by all means."

Gerald saw weariness suddenly descend on the old man, and on finishing his drink, tactfully made the excuse of another engagement, and left. As he crossed the silent, echoing hall, he looked round regretfully at the graceful curve of the staircase. The door of the drawing room was open. He paused for a moment, visualising bright lights, a leaping fire on the hearth, flowers and a crowd of guests. . . . Then, shaking off futile regrets, he let himself out, and got into his car.

Back at Edge Crescent, he carefully locked away Sir Miles LeWarne's will, and drove off again to have dinner with friends.

As a grass widower he had received numerous offers of

hospitality, and on Sunday both lunched and dined out. It was nearly midnight when he returned home, and he was surprised to hear the telephone ringing as he came in.

"Corbury 5687," he said, taking up the receiver.

"That you, Stanton? Lang here," came his doctor's familiar voice. "I've been trying to get you for the last couple of hours. Old LeWarne's had a stroke."

"Good God!" Gerald exclaimed in astonished dismay, instantly thinking of the unsigned will. "How bad is he? How incapacitated, I mean?"

"The left side's paralysed all the way down. His speech isn't too bad. A bit slurred, but quite intelligible. That's why I'm ringing you at this ungodly hour. The old boy's worrying about signing his will, and I promised him I'd get on to you."

"We'd got the signing all lined up for tomorrow morning. I was going over. . . . Is there a chance that he'll recover to any extent?"

"The outlook's not very promising at his age, and of course there could be another stroke at any time. But at the moment there's a fairly normal movement in the right arm and hand, and he could perfectly well sign his name. Is that all he's got to do?"

Gerald Stanton had a sensation, as much physical as mental, of an abrupt translation into an entirely new context, at the same time unknown and frighteningly explicit.

"Hallo?" came Doctor Lang's voice across infinity.

"Yes, I'm still here." To Gerald his own voice seemed to be functioning independently of himself. Could it conceivably sound normal, he wondered? "I was just reviewing the situation from the legal angle. Yes, all he's got to do is sign his name."

". . . oughtn't to be any difficulty, provided he goes on as he is at the moment," Doctor Lang was saying. "There'll be a nurse around. I've had the devil's own job getting hold of a couple, I can tell you. I had to—"

"Look here, Lang," he cut in abruptly. "This is a dicey situation for me, you know. Is there the slightest question of Sir Miles not being *compos mentis*?"

"None whatever. His mind is as clear as yours or mine. I'd be prepared to state it on oath, and so would Maggie Marsh, I'm certain."

"All the same, I'd like you to be there tomorrow morning

in your professional capacity for a last minute check-up on this."

"Oh, all right. I'll be along—I take your point. Could we say ten-thirty? I ought to be able to clear my surgery by then. One other thing. Could you face going over now for a word with Maggie Marsh? She's pretty badly tensed-up. Says she must sit up all night in case anything's wanted, and whatever. It'll be dashed awkward if she cracks up: he'd be wretched in a nursing home."

"Yes, he would. All right. I'll go along and try to calm her down. Thanks for ringing—sorry you had a job to get on to me. Be seeing you tomorrow morning, then."

They rang off. Gerald Stanton slumped down at his desk, staring unseeingly in front of him Doctor Lang's words continued to pulsate in his mind . . . is that all he has to do? . . . all . . . all . . . all . . . !

His thoughts were in turmoil. Part of his being reacted in horror at the idea of turning a client's incapacitating illness to personal advantage: the mere idea was a nightmarish fantasy. How could such a thing have entered his mind for a single moment? But at a deeper level, and gathering momentum, was his realization of the terrifying simplicity of the situation which had arisen. So dazzlingly simple to present a substituted will for the old man's signature tomorrow, in which Shirley, and not the Borough of Corbury was designated the residuary legatee of the estate. The element of risk? Even apart from the effects of the stroke, and Doctor Lang's poor prognosis, the likelihood of Sir Miles's ever asking to see his will again was less than negligible. He was a man who, having acted on a decision, almost tended to lose interest. If this had been characteristic of him in health, how much more would it be now?

Gerald Stanton planted his elbows on the desk, and pressed his fingers against his forehead. Once he had returned from seeing Maggie Marsh, the whole of the rest of the night lay before him in which to draft and type out a substitute will. Nothing could have been more useful than Doctor Lang's request that he should go over now to Edgehill Court. It was vital to the substitution plan that the copy of the unsigned genuine will should be removed from Sir Miles's desk tonight. The drawer in which he had been instructed to put it had been unlocked. Maggie? Gerald considered Maggie Marsh, and finally dismissed the idea of her having investigated her employer's private papers. He had known her for over ten years in her present post: she was just not that sort of woman. But she had daily help, and there were strange nurses in the house now. Obviously he must act tonight. Somehow he must ensure that he talk to Maggie in the study, and get her out of the room for as long as possible.

He got out his car and started off for Edgehill Court like an automaton, his thoughts wholly absorbed by these and other practical considerations. Suddenly, as he drove along the deserted ridge road, the significance of this preoccupation was borne in on him, and horror at himself overwhelmed him. In a flash, however, his mind provided an antidote. Of course, he reasoned, Uncle Miles was a very old man suffering the after-effects of an appalling shock. Roger LeWarne, destined to carry on the family tradition of involvement with Corbury, was dead. Perfectly understandable that Uncle Miles could now think of nothing but compensating the town for its loss, and had taken the shortest cut to this end. Had he been his normal balanced self, he could not have failed to see that the best solution was to instal his god-daughter, Corbury born and bred, at the Court in Roger's place.

The idea was convincing, and proliferated rapidly. By the time Gerald drew up outside Edgehill Court it had established itself in his thinking.

Maggie Marsh let him in, a pathetic figure with her tear-stained face and bulbous eyes full of anxiety. To his satisfaction she led him unhesitatingly to the study. The unattended fire had sunk to a heap of grey ash, and she hastily dragged forward an electric heater. Once they had sat down, the flood gates of her speech were opened.

"It's good of you to come, Mr. Stanton," she repeated. "It's not that I wouldn't do anything in the world for Sir Miles, as God knows. But it's the responsibility—feeling there's not a relative to turn to, now that Mr. Roger's gone."

"But Maggie, you've got me to turn to," Gerald reassured her. "I should have been here hours ago if Doctor Lang had been able to contact me: I was out for the evening, you see. You know that I'm Sir Miles's solicitor. He has put all his affairs in my hands, and I can deal with any problem that comes along. You've only to ring the office during working hours, and my house in the evenings. And I'll look in regularly."

She released a long unsteady sigh.

"Oh, sir, that's a real weight off my mind. It's been the thinking about what I'd do if he were to go. . . ."

"If Sir Miles died, all the necessary arrangements would be my responsibility. But from what Doctor Lang said to me just now, I don't think we need take quite such a gloomy view, you know, Maggie. In fact, he assured me that Sir Miles would be perfectly capable of signing his will tomorrow as arranged, so I'll be over again at half-past ten."

Skilfully he led the conversation on to practical details such as the arrangements for household expenses. Presently he glanced up at the clock. Maggie Marsh gave a start.

"Oh, sir," she exclaimed, "and I've never thought to ask you if you'd care for anything, and at this hour of the night, too!"

"Well, now you mention it," he said, smiling at her, "I could do with a cuppa and a sandwich. It seems a long time since supper."

"I'll get you a nice little snack right away sir," she told him, and immediately hurried out of the room.

Perfect, he thought, that the suggestion which left him alone in the room should come from her. . . . He was over at the desk in a flash, pulling open the bottom left-hand drawer. He scrutinized it intently, and was positive that its contents had not been touched. He remembered, when he had put in the copy of the original will, how he had slipped it under a folder, and one corner had projected slightly. He swiftly extracted the will and put it into the pocket of his sheepskin car coat. Then he made a rapid examination of the contents of the other drawers. Everything was orderly: classified receipts, insurance policies, reports of charitable organizations, unused stationery. . . . All quite impersonal. No unanswered letters, no notes on the proposed changes in the will. The memory of Sir Miles throwing his rough list of revised legacies into the fire returned reassuringly. He looked carefully all round the room and returned to his chair as sounds heralding Maggie's reappearance came from the hall.

A quarter of an hour later he was on his way home. The absolute ease with which his immediate aims had been fulfilled produced in him an almost hypnotic sense of destiny moving inevitably to fulfilment. But ahead of him were some hours of concentrated work. The actual drafting of the will to be substituted for the original presented little difficulty. The legacies were unaltered, except that Shirley's name must be removed from the list. Then, instead of the clauses dealing with the bequest to Corbury Borough Council, there must be a much briefer section designating her as residuary legatee. Care was needed here. It was important that the new will should appear to have roughly the same number of pages as the old. The elderly and the sick were sometimes surprisingly observant of detail. . . .

It was nearly five when all was finished. Gerald stood up, stretching his cramped limbs. In spite of the central heating, traces of the damp cold of the November night had seeped into the closely curtained room, and he felt chilled. Bracing himself for a final effort, he tore the two copies of the genuine will and the rough notes of the redrafting he had been doing into tiny pieces. These he disposed of in the downstairs lavatory, flushing the cistern twice. Finally he put the two copies of the substituted will into his brief case with some other papers, poured himself out a stiff whisky which he swallowed neat, and went upstairs to bed to snatch a couple of hours' sleep in what remained of the night. As he undressed he found himself convinced that he was doing for Sir Miles what the old man would obviously have done himself, had he been in his normal state of mind.

He awoke to find the same conviction dominant in his mind, and it was further strengthened by the matter-of-fact reaction of his young partner to the news of Sir Miles's stroke, and the impending signing of the will. For a brief moment on the drive over to Edgehill Court he panicked, visited by a horrific flash in which he saw himself discovered, ruined and imprisoned. But the casual question of one of his clerks about a wholly different matter dispelled the nightmare, and the sight of Dr. Lang's car parked in the drive restored the invincible certainty that everything was working out according to plan, because Shirley's inheriting had been meant to happen.

Sir Miles's bedroom was full of morning sunlight. Doctor Lang, standing by the bed, was breezy.

"Oh, here you are, Stanton," he said. "My patient's in fine form this morning."

Unexpectedly finding it more of an effort than he had expected, Gerald went to the bedside. The slightly distorted mouth managed a smile.

"Glad to see you, my boy," it said, thickly but intelligibly.

"Very sorry about this, Uncle Miles. We'll soon have you up and doing, though."

"Of course we shall," interposed Doctor Lang. "Now then, nurse, if the pillows are raised just a bit. . . . There's a table over there for you witness chaps to write at."

The nurse dealt with the pillows. The two clerks retreated to the far side of the room, and stood watching awkwardly. Gerald Stanton opened his briefcase and extracted the will which he had typed in the small hours. By a judicious spacing he had contrived that there was little besides the preamble to the testator's signature on the last page. He folded back the overlying pages.

"I've filled in the date, Uncle Miles," he said. "Here's your own pen, so if you'll just sign your name here, while the witnesses look on . . ."

He helped the nurse steady the blotter. The signature was unexpectedly firm.

"That's done," the twisted mouth said, more distinctly this time. "Don't forget copy in my desk. Look after 'em both. I don't want to bother—any—more."

"I'll do that thing," Gerald assured him, and took the document across to the two witnesses.

A few minutes later he was walking downstairs in the euphoria of things falling into place for him like the conclusion of a well-rung peal of bells. There followed, with complete naturalness, a short conversation with Doctor Lang before the latter hurried off, and some reassuring words with Maggie in the intimacy of the kitchen. Finally came the visit to the study to collect the copy of the will at Sir Miles's request.

On returning to the office he was at once immersed in the morning's business held up by the visit to Edgehill Court. At lunch time he sent out for sandwiches and ate them in the solitude of his room, in the atmosphere of slight unreality that characterizes a return to normal routine after a holiday. He considered at length what he should say to Shirley. Most fortunately, as he had told Sir Miles, she had an unusual sense of professional propriety. Her speculations would be kept to herself. He decided to talk freely about the signing of the will, and intimate that eventually it would make a difference to her.

She had promised to ring him as soon as she arrived home in the afternoon, and each time a call was put through to him he expected to hear her voice. At a quarter to four the buzzer went again.

"Doctor Lang would like to speak to you, Mr. Stanton," his secretary told him.

Suddenly taut, he picked up the receiver.

"Stanton speaking," he said.

"Lang here. LeWarne's gone. In his sleep, half an hour ago."

# Chapter 3

Bernard Lister learnt of Sir Miles LeWarne's death on the following Saturday from the *Corbury Courier*. The news was splashed across the front page and there was a leader entitled THE END OF AN ERA FOR CORBURY. He was surprised at his sense of personal loss. Probing into it he decided that his reaction underlined the unhappiness of his early years in the town. If life in the Plowman household had been even moderately happy, the occasional kindnesses of Sir Miles would hardly stand out like beacons in his memory.

At once he began to regret the diffidence which had deterred him from keeping in touch with his benefactor. The familiar sense of his ineptitude in personal relationships descended on him like a black cloud. As he read the lengthy obituary, a reference to Shirley Stanton as the deceased's godchild infuriated him.

"Bitch," he muttered. "The old chap never meant a bloody thing to her."

The thought that Shirley would almost certainly have been left a legacy added fuel to the flames. He sat clenching and unclenching his hands, his lips drawn back unpleasantly. Suddenly he shouted aloud a string of abusive epithets, which seemed to hang and vibrate in the air around him. Then, as always after one of his emotional storms, he felt degraded, and sank into self-depreciation.

Presently, in an effort to rally himself, he picked up the *Courier* again. The sight of the most recent list of subscribers to the Millenary Fund was a welcome distraction. He had by no means abandoned his intention of looking into the authenticity of the Corbury charters. At the moment he was fully occupied with the proofs of his forthcoming book on the post-Conquest agriculture in England, and a series of articles for one of the historical journals. But he should be relatively free after Easter, and the Millenary was still nearly two years ahead.

His book was published at Easter, and its favourable reception in academic circles was a tonic to his self-confidence. He took the busy summer term in his stride, and allowed himself a fortnight's austere but pleasurable holiday, spent in visiting lesser-known Romanesque churches in France. Refreshed by this break, he returned to his flat in Warhampton and took up the researches on Corbury with renewed zest.

He was now concentrating on the text of the charters, and soon found that the first recorded enrolment, or official registration in Chancery of these, dated only from 1450. This enrolment cited a series of earlier charters from the thirteenth century onwards, but none of these had been registered. Bernard Lister was highly elated to find this suggestion of possible forgery by Corbury burgesses of the fifteenth century, anxious to obtain such rights as quittance of their feudal dues, and exemption from tolls on the sale of merchandise.

Following a hunch, he looked up the texts of the charters granted to other towns by Henry I and his successors, and immediately made a breakthrough. He discovered that those of the county town of Allchester were almost identical in wording with those cited in the Corbury enrolment of 1450, even to the names of the witnesses. The correspondence was so overwhelming that he could hardly believe his eyes. He was well aware that perfectly genuine charters often included clauses copied from those of other towns, but surely the Corbury–Allchester situation went far beyond this? Was it possible, he speculated, that the men of fifteenth century Corbury could really have got away with it? He came to the conclusion that they could. It was a period of political confusion arising from the York–Lancaster rivalries. Chancery clerks had been demonstrably slack over checking previous enrolments in other cases. And of course there was the obvious explanation of bribery, both at Allchester and in London.

So far so good, he thought, but to commit himself to taking the matter up publicly he would need practically incontrovertible evidence. He had no intention of sticking his neck out. He decided to go down to Allchester and spend the last week of the vacation in studying the originals of both the towns' charters.

On the following day he made the journey by car, and put up at an hotel in Allchester's cathedral close. The City Archi-

vist, an elderly man, was welcoming and there was a flatter-
ing touch of respect in his comments on *Agricultural Changes
in Post-Conquest England*. The City Records Office was quiet
and well-found, and every facility for Bernard Lister's investigations was made available: the atmosphere was congenial.
Before he settled down to work he wandered around, scrutinizing the shelves, delighted by the wealth of historical material. Parish registers, deeds, wills . . . mute witnesses of
generations of human happiness and misery, with unrecog-
nized consequences stemming right down the centuries into
the present, he thought.

Presently he established himself at a secluded table and
carefully extracted a small packet wrapped in soft paper from
an envelope bearing an index number. Inside it was a folded
parchment. Allchester's first charter, granted by Henry I in
1110. It was exquisitely inscribed in the Chancery hand of
the period, in the fadeless medieval ink compounded of oak
gall and iron. The parchment was discoloured, but perfectly
legible, and the cords from which the impression of the Great
Seal of England had been lost, still bore traces of the wax.
With a touch of emotion Bernard Lister began to study the
wording of the document.

It was on his third day in the Records Office that the
Archivist came along to enquire into his progress, and stood
looking over his shoulder at papers on the table.

"I see you're just starting on the Allchester Edward III,"
he said. "That's the one that vandal John Todd had the
effrontery to emend. Look at that!"

He pointed to a superimposed alteration of a personal
name, and a margin note in faded blue ink.

"Who was the blighter?" Bernard Lister asked indignantly.

"A nineteenth-century amateur historian of this city. He
seems to have spent his time delving into the records of local
families, and discovered that the name of the witness given
as Robertus le Skinner should have been 'le Spinner.' The
clerk who wrote out the charter obviously made a slip, and
it got by. So Todd waded in, and staked a claim to immortality
on a signed note in the margin. We were curious about the
alteration a year or two ago, and tried the violet lamp
on it."

Bernard Lister caught his breath.

"Hold on a minute," he said, and reached for the Corbury

charter of 1450. . . . "My God, it's 'Robertus le Skinner' in this one!"

The Archivist whistled.

"You're as home and dry as you'll ever be, aren't you?"

Like many insecure people Bernard Lister over-reacted to success as well as to failure. After entertaining the clearly impressed City Archivist to lunch he left Allchester feeling exhilarated, his mood intensified by the cloudless sky and mellow sunshine of a perfect autumn afternoon. Suddenly he was seized with the astonishing idea of making a detour to Corbury. Twenty years ago he had sworn to himself never to enter the place again. . . . He debated, and found the prospect of strolling in its streets, conscious of now being able to debunk its absurd pretensions, quite irresistible. His foot increased its pressure on the accelerator. A few miles further on, and with a sense of unreality at his action, he took a right fork.

He drove fast, and the relentless Roman road fell away rapidly behind him. Soon, with an irritating slight constriction at his heart, he saw the distant blur on the edge of the downs which was Corbury. All too swiftly the blur resolved itself into the familiar skyline dominated by the tower of St. Gundryth's Church, and the variegated spill of buildings down the scarp into the plain below. He could see that the town had expanded appreciably at this lower level. Now he could pick out Plowman's Pottery, and wondered with sudden savagery how that beefy oaf Mark was making out. One thing was certain: the traffic was ten times what it used to be. He ground up High Street in bottom gear in the wake of an oil tanker . . . shops, some familiar, more new and brash . . . where best to park? Remembering the spacious forecourt of St. Gundryth's he turned right at the top of the hill but found closely packed lines of cars in front of the church. As he hesitated a man drove out, and he hastily ran his car into the vacant space.

He got out and stood looking about him, puzzled that there seemed to be so much more open ground than formerly. Then he remembered reading in the *Courier* that the former church school, a grim Gothic fortress, had been demolished, and that Roman remains were discovered beneath it. Quite extensive excavations seemed to be in progress. Bernard Lister walked across to investigate, and was interested. The greater part of the foundations of a large Roman villa had been uncovered, and small areas under tarpaulins suggested tessellated pavements. Investigations were now going on beyond the villa, in the area to the south-east, where trial trenches had been dug. The whole site was cordoned off, and bristled with deterrent notices to the public on behalf of the County Archaeological Society. In the absence of any workers, Bernard Lister disregarded these, and slipped under the rope barriers for a closer look. He decided that the whole complex had been one of some importance, obviously related to the Roman road along which he had just driven. The historian in him was intrigued, but at the same time it was exasperating that the wretched town could now claim the distinction of a Roman settlement on its site, however spurious its medieval charters were.

He had now reached the limit of the dig, and stood looking up at the backs of the houses in Edge Crescent, experiencing once again that slight, but disagreeable inner sensation. . . . There was the window of the small north-facing bedroom on the second floor which had been allotted to him in the Plowmans' house. He stood staring up at it, self-pity, anger and triumph contending in his mind. Then he turned away with an abrupt movement, retracing his steps and walking in the direction of the High Street, thrusting down the uncomfortable fact that old fears and inhibitions were reasserting themselves. Remembering a second-hand bookshop which had been one of the refuges of his youth, he walked a short distance down the hill to see if it had survived. On his way he came to a new estate agency, its window full of particulars of properties and forthcoming sales. The words EDGEHILL COURT caught his eye, and he stopped to read further.

BALDWIN & YOUNG'S AUCTION ROOMS
3 CORNMARKET,
ALLCHESTER

Important Sale of furniture and effects, including lots from EDGEHILL COURT, residence of the late Sir Miles LeWarne, Bart, on

FRIDAY, 29 SEPTEMBER, 1972.

Sale commences 10:00 a.m. promptly. Viewing the previous day 10:00 a.m.–5:00 p.m.

A wave of nostalgia engulfed Bernard Lister as he visualized the break up and dispersal of the home which had symbolized to him the ideal way of life: secure, recognized and cultured. He resolved instantly to change his plans and attend the sale on the following day, in the hopes that something which he remembered from Sir Miles LeWarne's study would be included. He would have it, whatever it cost, if necessary getting rid of furniture of his own to make room for it in the flat. As these thoughts passed through his mind, the face of a young girl was briefly mirrored in the plate glass window. It was vaguely familiar . . . a student? As he turned to look at the girl's back as she went on up the street, he found a sharp-faced man in a baggy blue suit standing beside him.

"Thinkin' of goin' over to the sale ter-morrow, Guv?" this individual inquired. "You won't find none of the good stuff from the Court there, and that's a fac'. The lady'll've cottoned on to all that."

"The lady?"

"Thasright. Mrs. Stanton, wife of old LeeWorn's lawyer up yonder. Town Clerk, 'e is, too. Fair scooped the pool, she did, seein' the old gent 'adn't no relatives left. 'Is goddaughter, she was—there weren't none of 'is family livin', not after a nevvy or some such was killed in a car smash. All in the *Courier*, it was, sayin' 'ow 'e'd left 'er the Court, an' a packet, too, last Friday's . . ."

Belinda Plowman found her mother reclining on a chaise longue in the summer-house, reading a glossy magazine.

"Guess what, Mummy," she said, flopping down on a neighbouring chair and shaking her hair out of her eyes. "I've just seen Blister. Here, in Corbury, glued to the window of Baldwin & Young's. I'm certain it was him. I wish now I'd accosted him. How would he have reacted, do you think?"

Monica Plowman was so startled that the magazine slipped to the floor.

"I don't think it could possibly have been him," she said, in a tone which suggested an attempt at self-reassurance. "He's never been back since he came into his money, and treated granny and grandpa so disgracefully. Don't mention it to—"

"Daddy," Belinda cut in, with a grin. "O.K., Mummy, I'll spare his feelings. He'll be a bit jaded when he gets back from Cornwall tonight, poor pet! But it *was* Blister—I'd swear to it. After all, I sat gooping at him all through a lecture last autumn. Perhaps he's thinking of buying a house here," she added mischievously. "Shall I make some tea, and bring it out here?"

"Yes do, darling. I'm longing for a cup. And bring what's left of the chocolate cake. It's in the blue tin."

Belinda stood up and stretched, agreeably aware of her slenderness.

"You really shouldn't, Mummy. You're heading for Weight-watchers," she said, surveying her mother's comfortable plumpness.

"I only had one potato at lunch," Monica protested plaintively.

Belinda grinned.

"On your head be it," she said. "Only it won't be your head, will it? Your tail, more like: middle-age spread."

She went off in the direction of the house. This last fort-night of her summer vacation was being dutifully spent at home, and time was hanging a little heavily on her hands. As she drank her tea, she decided to divert herself by reporting Blister's presence in Corbury to her Aunt Shirley, and watch how she reacted.

The Stantons' changed attitude to the Plowman family since the death of Sir Miles LeWarne had been a source of sardonic amusement to Belinda. They had obviously decided that, despite their deficiencies, Mark and Monica must be fully incorporated into their own enhanced status as owners of Edgehill Court. In actual fact, the *rapprochement* with Mark had been heavy going. Finally, Gerald Stanton invented an alleged verbal request to Shirley by Sir Miles to modernize the equipment of his old friend's Pottery. After satisfying himself that no strings were attached to the offer, Mark had accepted. This development also led to a change in his bank manager's attitude. Freed from immediate financial worry, he was able to concentrate on production, with encouraging results. Gerald Stanton's brainwave of contacting Corbury, U.S.A. in connection with the Millenary Celebrations, had met with an enthusiastic response, and a substantial order for souvenirs had already come in. Meanwhile Shirley had addressed herself to cultivating her hitherto despised sister-in-law. Monica Plowman, who above all liked life to run smoothly and pleasantly, accepted her overtures uncritically.

Belinda, who had never been in doubt about her aunt's

business acumen, collected together some of her own designs for pottery jugs and beakers as a pretext for her visit. Shirley was in and received her warmly.

"Nice of you to look in, my dear," she said.

"Are you madly busy?" Belinda asked. "I've brought along a few designs I'd like your opinion on."

"I'm only too glad of an excuse to knock off. Actually, there's a bit of a lull now that the Court stuff has gone off to the sale room. It couldn't be taken out of the house until probate was granted, of course, but I've been sorting and listing for months. And we've been making all the decisions about modernizing and redecorating, and so on."

"When will you move in?" Belinda asked.

"In the New Year, I hope. Everything always takes so much longer than you expect. The whole place has got to be rewired, to start with. Show me these designs of yours."

Belinda handed them over and watched her aunt appraise them critically.

"You've got what it takes, you know," Shirley Stanton remarked. "This jug, for instance, would definitely be a good selling line at a reasonable profit. Try to get your father to put it into production right away. . . . How many generations of Plowman potters do you make?"

"Five, I think. No, six, isn't it, counting old Obadiah and his butter crocks in the late seventeen hundreds? Talking about the family, who do you think I saw in High Street this afternoon? That cousin who was brought up with you and Daddy. Bernard Lister."

Shirley Stanton looked at her in blank astonishment.

"But have you met him?"

Belinda explained once again about the lecture she had attended.

"Oh, well, if you've only seen him on a platform. . . . It's not at all likely that he'd honour Corbury with a visit, you know. It was probably someone unfortunate enough to look like him—rather ape-like. Now, reverting to this jug of yours . . ."

Rather elaborately unconcerned, Belinda wondered, as she strolled home later on? On the whole she thought that her aunt had been genuinely uninterested. Probably her mother was living in the past over the Plowman attitude to Blister.

Shirley Stanton had, however, been sufficiently interested to retail Belinda's story to her husband when he came home.

Gerald paused fractionally. A lightning check on the possible relevance of unexpected news to the affairs of Sir Miles LeWarne had become a habit with him. He was reassured.

"Fifty to one against Blister showing up in Corbury, don't you think?" he replied.

"Just about. I hope Belinda won't take it into her head to cultivate him, though. A pity they're both at Warhampton."

"I shouldn't imagine any advances from her would be reciprocated. After all, she's Mark's daughter. By the way, Mike Baldwin rang about something this afternoon, and said there was a good crowd at the preview."

In fact, attendance was so good that the previewing period was extended, and Bernard Lister found the auction rooms still open on his return to Allchester. Taut with fury at the thought of Shirley Stanton established at Edgehill Court, he nevertheless pursued his objective of buying something which had been in the study at the time of his visit there. To his satisfaction the desk was on sale. It was not a valuable antique, merely a well-made Victorian piece in mahogany, unlikely to be earmarked by wealthy dealers. Bernard tried the drawers which ran like satin, and fingered the little balustrade which ran round three sides of the top. It was as good as his. . . .

Nothing else evoked memories for him except the books. They had lined the whole of one wall, their handsome bindings creating a delectable atmosphere of intellectual opulence. As he inspected the various lots he smiled a little wryly. Their almost mint condition suggested that perhaps Sir Miles had not made all that much use of his library. He decided to bid for a fine edition of Gibbon's *Decline and Fall of the Roman Empire*, and some runs of the English classics to replace his own odd volumes.

He slept badly that night, tormented by the sense of the Plowmans' having invaded and taken over the one small corner of Corbury which, in a curious way, had become a part of his inmost self. He awoke unrefreshed, to find that his enthusiasm for the sale had largely evaporated. However, he attended it, and eventually secured the various lots he wanted without difficulty. Then, having arranged for their despatch to Warhampton, he left the town once again, this time accelerating to shoot past the Corbury fork. He was very tired, ashamed of having been so churned up emotionally, and the prospect of going to ground in his flat seemed the only thing that mattered. The road unreeled endlessly ahead, and it was dark as he reached the outskirts of Warhampton.

He lived on the first floor of a house which had been converted into three select self-contained flats. Their rents were high, this being reflected in the well maintained hall and staircase. He let himself in, pausing a moment to relish his arrival. He was fortunate in his fellow tenants. Mrs. Tresillian on the second floor was a widow in her sixties, given to vapid small talk when encountered but otherwise innocuous. On the ground floor Dr. James Halton, a distinguished ornithologist, was seldom in residence, spending much of his time on expeditions to remote areas, or in attending conferences, accompanied by his wife as amanuensis. As there was no light showing on their premises Bernard Lister concluded that they were probably away at the moment.

In his own flat everything was in order, just as he had left it. Once a week a woman came in to clean, under his eye: he would not have dreamt of handing over the key to anyone. Otherwise he fended competently for himself. Progressively more relaxed, he began to unpack in a leisurely way. Presently it occurred to him that he was thinking about his discovery in the Allchester archives instead of dwelling on the new situation at Edgehill Court. Why, he asked himself in a moment of sudden illumination, should he allow Shirley to poison his life once again? His eye fell on the previous week's *Corbury Courier*, still in its wrapper . . . it's all in last week's *Courier*, the man outside the estate agency had said. . . .

He snatched up the packet, went into his kitchen, and dropped it into the rubbish chute. The fraction of a second later it landed with a hollow thud in the dustbin below.

The first weeks of the autumn term were unexpectedly agreeable. Bernard Lister found his stock remaining high as his book met with continued success. He contrived to group his lectures and tutorials to allow himself more time than usual for research and writing. He discovered promising material among his first-year students. His purchases arrived from Allchester, and the desk was installed to his complete satisfaction. The books were stacked in the spare bedroom awaiting an enjoyable reorganization of his entire library in the next vacation.

Checking his new data on the Corbury charters meant visits to the Public Record Office. By spending a Friday night in London, and returning to Warhampton on Saturday evening he thought that he could cover a satisfactory amount of ground. He came home from such a visit in a state of mild euphoria, aware that his paper on the charters was shaping very well. It was a sharp clear evening after a rainy day, and he decided to walk from the station instead of taking a taxi. He strode along preoccupied, casting and recasting a key paragraph, so absorbed that he was surprised to find that he had arrived on his doorstep. He let himself in mechanically, and it took the state of the normally immaculate hall to jerk him into the present. The floor was a mass of muddy footmarks which continued up the stairs, while scraps of paper and an empty cigarette carton were strewn around. He stared blankly, and then concluded that Mrs. Tresillian must have workmen in. As he went up to his flat it struck him as odd that they should start on a job on a Saturday.

He had hardly set down his case when there was a crash overhead, followed by a muffled shout. He had always sedulously avoided becoming involved with Mrs. Tresillian, but after a moment's hesitation felt obliged to investigate, and went up to the second floor. A knock on the door produced no answer, but he thought he could hear movement inside, and pushed up the flap of the letter box.

"Everything all right up here, Mrs. Tresillian?" he called. "It's Bernard Lister."

He registered frowsty tobacco smoke and a hurried confabulation. Then steps approached and the door was opened by a young man with shoulder-length blond hair wearing a purple tunic over grubby fawn trousers. He was barefooted, and eyed Bernard Lister with reserve.

"Mrs. Tresillian's abroad till Easter," he said, with an unexpected public school accent. "I'm her nephew, David Tresillian. She's lent me this flat while she's away. Sorry if we disturbed you. A box of books went over."

Seeing Bernard Lister's incredulous expression he added that he was second year at the University, reading sociology.

Inside the flat another figure leant against the doorpost of the sitting room with a kind of insolent languor, at the same time attentively listening to the conversation. From the room itself came the provocative twanging of a guitar, and some brief flourishes on a drum. There was unmistakable hostility in the air. Bernard Lister responded by taking the offensive.

"How many of you are proposing to live in this flat?" he demanded.

David Tresillian stiffened. The figure in the doorway was joined by another.

"Hardly your business, whoever you are."

"On the contrary, it's decidedly my business. I'm a member of the University myself, and my work needs reasonable peace and quiet. Mrs. Tresillian may have lent this place to you personally, but I refuse to believe that she intended it to be turned into a students' hostel."

The immediate reaction to this speech took him by surprise. The two figures inside melted silently away. The guitar and the drum were abruptly silenced. David Tresillian stared at him, his mouth slightly open.

"You mean you're one of the dons?"

"I am. Bernard Lister, Reader in Medieval History."

There was a pregnant silence. Then David Tresillian became incoherently defensive. It was bloody unfair to take it for granted that students always made a filthy row . . . anyway, they'd thought the other tenants were all away . . . if people objected to students in the house, why didn't the University build more flats for them? . . . four chaps could hardly help making a bit more row than one elderly person, but they were perfectly ready to try to pipe down within reason. . . .

"I'm glad to have your assurance on this, Mr. Tresillian," Bernard Lister cut in coldly. "Good night."

He returned to his own flat conscious of having had the last word, and still astonished at the effect his status appeared to have produced, but utterly appalled by the threat to his peaceful existence. From a long experience of students his imagination built up rowdy parties thundering overhead, with pop music blaring into the small hours and beyond, noisy cars revving their engines and repeatedly having their doors slammed, and continual shouting and tramping on the stairs. In actual fact his new neighbours were surprisingly quiet, but he spent a wretched evening anticipating the next sound from above. Surely, he argued with himself, the clause in his lease which prohibited subletting would also be in Mrs. Tresillian's?

At the earliest possible moment on Monday morning he rang the agent employed by the owner of the house, who was voluble in his disapproval of the students' occupation, but regretfully informed him that nothing could be done about it.

"All the advance notice we had was a letter from Mrs.

Tresillian which arrived *after* her departure on this world tour, Mr. Lister, simply stating that she had given her nephew permission to occupy the premises in her absence as her guest. This is it, you see, Mr. Lister: no money changing hands, so technically it's not subletting. We—"

"But the fact that she's lent him the flat surely doesn't mean that he's entitled to pack out the place with his friends?"

The agent embarked on a long statement about the right to exercise hospitality, always provided that no public nuisance was involved, and the obvious impracticability of taking legal action under the circumstances, unless there was damage to the property, for which Mrs. Tresillian would, of course, be responsible to the owner.

"Of course, if the disturbance *does* become a public nuisance, Mr. Lister, you and Dr. Halton would be in a position to make a complaint to the police. I can't say how much we regret . . ."

During the following days Bernard Lister was obliged to recognize that the students were doing nothing that could be held to constitute a public nuisance. At the same time the increased traffic on the stairs and overhead fretted his nerves, and the muted, but still audible, pop music drove him to frenzy. Intolerable though it was to be driven from his home, he decided to spend both Friday and Saturday nights in London. He came back in a mood of black depression, the hideous prospect of the months ahead looming grimly, and did not notice that there were lights in the windows of the ground floor flat. As he came in, its front door opened to reveal the towering bulk of Dr. Halton, his red hair and beard even more dishevelled than usual.

"That you, Lister?" he said. "Come in, for God's sake, and tell us what the hell's happening in old Mother Tresillian's flat."

Inside was chaos. Papers, cameras, film tapes and miscellaneous packages littered the sitting room.

"Afraid I'm in a bit of a mess," James Halton understated, sweeping the contents of a couple of chairs on the floor. "Sit down, and I'll get drinks. Peggy's still in London. We only got back from the Bosporus on Friday. Storks," he added, by way of explanation, and headed for the kitchen.

In a short space of time he reappeared carrying two glasses and a siphon of soda water, a bottle of whisky under one arm.

"Say when," he invited. "Splash? Right. Cheers! Now, let's have the gen."

Bernard Lister, who always felt at a disadvantage on account of the ornithologist's formidable physique and abounding vitality, gave a slightly pedantic résumé of the situation.

"Apparently," he concluded, "there's nothing to be done. We're simply stuck with these yobs till Mrs. T. elects to come back."

James Halton drained his glass with gusto, and set it down. He stared at Bernard Lister with good-humoured amusement.

"Man," he said, "take courage, as the advert says. Can it be you didn't notice the stink in the place when you came in from God's fresh air just now?"

"It was a bit frowsty, certainly," Bernard Lister replied defensively. "I expect the flat's filthy already."

"Frowst and filth my foot! They threw a party on Friday night, and the whole house reeked of pot. It's still hanging about. Never come across it before? Well, well! Better leave it to me to take the obvious steps, then."

At midweek a brief note pushed through his letterbox informed Bernard Lister that everything was going according to plan. Uneasiness descended upon him. Did this mean a raid by the police, and getting involved in undesirable publicity? If Halton was right about the pot, it explained the consternation the students had shown on discovering that they were living above a member of the University staff. He remembered running into David Tresillian as he left the house for the station before lunch on Friday, carrying his overnight case. This could explain the party. Halton's return was something they couldn't have foreseen.

On Thursday evening he was summoned to James Halton's flat for a police briefing. Inspector Worrall of the Warhampton CID was a spare man of few words, whom Bernard Lister found reassuring. He learnt that David Tresillian and his friends were associating with a man known to the police as a suspected pusher of hard drugs as well as cannabis.

"Friday's the popular night for these parties among students," the Inspector said. "As I've just been saying to Dr. Halton, we'd like both of you to make yourselves scarce next Friday, giving the impression that you're away for the weekend if you can. We shall keep the house under observation, and if this chap we're interested in turns up, we'll probably go in ourselves."

"Anything you like," James Halton told him, "and I'm sure that goes for you, too, Lister, doesn't it? I've seen too much of where this sort of thing lands these young fools, if they once get hooked."

Relieved at the prospect of being able to contract out of a disturbance in the house, Bernard Lister replied that he would be glad to co-operate.

"How about eating together at a pub on Friday night, then? You could let us have a ring when you're either through, or have called it off, Inspector."

"That's a good plan," Inspector Worrall approved. "Which pub would you gentlemen fancy?"

"Grand Central suit you, Lister? We may as well have a decent meal while we're about it. It's bound to be a damned uncomfortable day."

Thankful at not being asked to patronize a noisy pub of the type he detested, Bernard Lister agreed willingly. The Grand Central was the best of the city's rather limited selection of hotels. Inspector Worrall assured them that they would not be kept out of their homes a moment longer than was necessary, and departed after thanking them for their help.

On the following morning Bernard Lister awoke with a sense of unreality. He set about playing the part assigned to him with his usual thoroughness, and at midday set off with a weekend case. Instead of going to the station for the London train, however, he took his car and drove some fifty miles to a small country town with an interesting church. After lunching he inspected the latter, and then spent the rest of the afternoon reading in the almost deserted lounge of the hotel, only returning to Warhampton in time to meet James Halton at the Grand Central. The evening with the ebullient ornithologist was less of an ordeal than he had anticipated. In fact, he enjoyed himself. The food and wine were good, and his companion intelligent, if highly individualistic.

They had moved to the hotel lounge for coffee and liqueurs when James Halton was called to the telephone.

"Operation successful," he reported on returning. "No details over the blower, of course, but we can go back when we like. Thank God we shan't have to repeat this performance every Friday night until further notice. You said you'd got your car here, didn't you?"

They left together shortly afterwards, and when Bernard Lister had garaged his car, walked round to the house. A police car was just driving away with a full complement of passengers. As they watched, David Tresillian and some other young men were conducted to another car. Finally another group of young people emerged under escort. As they got into a third car the light from the street lamp fell on the frightened face of a girl which touched off an elusive memory in Bernard Lister's mind. It was some hours later, just as he was dropping off to sleep, that he identified it with the reflection in the window of the estate agency at Corbury.

# Chapter 4

All through the traumatic experience of being taken to a police station and charged with smoking cannabis, Belinda Plowman's one thought was that her parents must never know. At all costs she must clamp down on her link with Corbury. When asked for information about herself, she stated with perfect truth that she was eighteen years old, legally of age, and that her private address was the flat in Warhampton which she shared with two other girls. At last she was released on bail in her own recognizances of ten pounds, badly shaken, but confident that she had given nothing away.

Although almost sick with exhaustion she could not sleep that night. At intervals she sweated in panic at the thought of her father's distress if he found out what had happened. She repeatedly tried to reassure herself with what she had heard of the fate of other people on drugs charges. Would the Bench ever believe that she had never in her life experimented with drugs before, and had only gone to Dave Tresillian's wretched party to take a trip out of sheer curiosity? Surely first offenders didn't get sent to prison these days? Money to pay a fine could be raised somehow. Would they let you pay in instalments? She'd ask Dave. Of course, things would be worse for him, because he'd let his flat be used for the party. Worse still for that friend of his who'd brought the stuff along . . . not that she'd taken to him at all. Oh, God, what a fool she'd been . . .

Belinda rolled over on to her back and stared into the darkness. If the police didn't know where she came from, she argued, it couldn't come out in court, and so the Press wouldn't be able to get hold of it.

This naïve belief showed her inexperience of the techniques of newsmen. Once the names of the students who had been charged were made public, it took a reporter on the *War-*

*hampton Evening News* very little time to uncover their various backgrounds through casual conversations with their acquaintances. The information so obtained began to circulate over the national Press network.

In the middle of the following week Bob Risley, editor of the *Corbury Courier*, rang Gerald Stanton at his office.

"Something a shade dicey's come in," he told him. "I thought I'd just check with you before contacting Plowman. I take it you're all in the picture over this drugs charge his girl's facing?"

In response to a curt request for information, Bob Risley replied that he had just taken the precaution of ringing the Warhampton police. Belinda Plowman and others were being hauled up before the Warhampton beaks on a cannabis smoking charge. The case was coming up in a week's time.

When he rang off, Gerald Stanton sat for a moment staring at his telephone. Whether Mark Plowman knew about it or not, the prospect of confronting him on the situation was daunting. Still, steps must be taken without delay to ensure that Belinda had a competent solicitor.

"Get me Mrs. Stanton," he said abruptly, pressing the buzzer on his desk.

Shirley Stanton used all her intelligence, and the full weight of her personality and status to influence Corbury's reaction to her niece's escapade. She anticipated small-town shocked reaction by discussing the situation openly, and deploring the type of student being maintained at universities on the taxpayers' money. She gave it as her private opinion that coming into contact with the law was not a bad thing to happen to a thoroughly decent girl like Belinda. The shock would make her choose her friends more critically in the future. Gerald Stanton put out similar sentiments in masculine terms. A sense of reacting in an enlightened way to an unfortunate occurrence began to permeate Corbury society.

To a stunned Monica Plowman the Stantons were sympathetic and cheerfully bracing. Mark, as Gerald had instantly foreseen, constituted a major hazard. It was only with great difficulty that he was deterred from plunging into catastrophic action on Belinda's behalf. He was at last persuaded that a personal onslaught on the young men who had organized the party would make her the laughing stock of her contemporaries. Cutting off her allowance in an attempt to make her leave

Warhampton for good might well lead to her walking out on the family: such reactions from the young were a commonplace these days. As a trump card Shirley quoted a local example. Reluctantly convinced that his proposed courses of action had better be abandoned, Mark remained adamant on one matter. He, and he only would represent the family when the case came up in court. A crowd of them there would only make it worse for the poor kid.

"All the same," Shirley said to her husband in private, "I do wish you were going to be there. Suppose Mark suddenly blows his top in public?"

"If he does, he does," Gerald replied irritably, exasperated by the whole business. "I can't possibly go, with a client's case on at Allchester on the same day. He'll be all right. You've hammered it in hard enough that it's in Belinda's interest for him to keep his cool."

In this Gerald Stanton was to be proved right. Mark Plowman was slow to accept an idea which cut across his inclinations, but having done so, he held to it tenaciously. He greeted Belinda on the day of her ordeal with cheerful composure. During the hearing of the case he concealed his agonies of apprehension and impatience, and his fury at the remarks addressed to the three girls prior to their discharge. Outside the court he moderated his heartfelt relief.

"How about tea at my hotel?" he suggested, and moved by an impulse of goodwill, he included the two other girls in the invitation. Belinda's glance of approval was ample reward for the sacrifice of their tête-à-tête.

In the hotel lounge, warm and brightly-lit, with its buzz of conversation against a background of canned popular music, tension rapidly evaporated. The trio tucked into crumpets and cakes with the resilience of youth. At first the events of the day were avoided, but before long they were being uninhibitedly discussed.

One of the girls, an undergraduate at Warhampton University, remarked that the chap who had snooped and reported to the police had not shown up in court.

"But do you know who it was?" Mark Plowman asked her. "The police usually keep mum about their sources of information."

"Oh, everyone says it was one of our lecturers," she assured him. "He had the flat under Dave Tresillian's. A dreary type from the history department, called Bernard Lister. I know him quite well by sight."

His teacup halfway to his lips, Mark Plowman was suddenly immobilized. An ugly brick red mounted swiftly to his temples. In a flash he saw alarm in Belinda's eyes, and decided to attempt reassurance.

"My God, it's hot in here," he exclaimed. "I feel like a boiled lobster. I suppose there'd be a riot if anybody asked for a window to be opened?"

As he spoke he beckoned to a passing waitress, and in the slight upheaval which followed the conversation took another turn, becoming progressively more lighthearted. Under its cover he felt the violent impulses so ruthlessly repressed for Belinda's sake turning to blind fury against Bernard Lister. A plan, nebulous at first, then alluringly explicit, took shape in his mind. But he must play for safety: she was uncommonly penetrating. When the tea-party ended he contrived, rather clumsily but doggedly, to be seen off in his car by all three girls.

The repercussions of David Tresillian's party had not extended far beyond Corbury. Simultaneously, there had been an exchange of radiograms between the agent for the flats and Mrs. Tresillian on her cruise ship in mid-Pacific. Its outcome was the precipitate departure of her nephew and his friends from her flat. Peace descended on the house once more.

To Bernard Lister this development was like an awakening from a nightmare. No longer tensed up in continual anticipation of the next disturbance, he found his flat more delectable than ever. He positively revelled in it, getting particular pleasure both from contemplating Sir Miles LeWarne's desk, and working at it. At the back of his mind the untidy stacks of books in his spare room began to irk him. His university work was keeping him fully occupied, but late one night he suddenly decided to make a start on reorganizing his bookshelves.

He began with his novels, and cleared a space for the editions of George Eliot and Trollope which he had bought at the sale. While he was carrying a pile of these into the sitting-room, several volumes slipped to the floor. He hastily set down the others and retrieved them, inspecting the bindings for any signs of damage. One book had fallen open at a place marked by a folded sheet of paper. It was *Framley Parsonage*, and on unfolding the paper Bernard Lister saw that it was a sheet of Edgehill Court stationery, covered with neat old-fashioned handwriting. He had exceptional visual memory, and at once recognized Sir Miles LeWarne's hand from the never-to-be forgotten cheque of many years ago. Interested, he sat down at the desk, and pulled an angle-poise lamp forward. The next moment his attention was riveted.

The paper was headed "Gerald Stanton. Final Notes for New Will. 5.12.1971." There were two sub-headings. Under the first, "Alterations to Legacies, etc." were annuities to Margaret Marsh and Thomas Bryce. There were bequests to various charities, and also to a few individuals, among them Shirley Stanton who received £5,000. Puzzled by this, as she had apparently inherited the bulk of the estate, Bernard Lister read the second section, which was headed "Residuary Estate."

Here several false starts had been made and crossed out, all of them containing the word "Corbury." The final version was a series of notes . . . "long association of my family with Corbury . . ." "to be perpetuated by town's ownership of E. Court and grounds in perpetuity . . ." "adequate endowment for upkeep . . ."

Bernard Lister read the document a second time before putting it down and sitting very still for some moments. Then his right hand felt for a drawer in the desk, opened it, and extracted some folders. He selected one of these, and pushed the others aside, immediately becoming absorbed in the *Corbury Courier*'s coverage of the deaths of the two young LeWarnes, and of Sir Miles. He had been sufficiently moved at the time to take cuttings, and in his usual methodical way had clipped them together in chronological order. His hand reached for a pen, and he began to jot down notes, as if assembling data in a piece of historical research.

Roger and Celia LeWarne had been killed on 20 November. Their ashes had been interred in Corbury churchyard on 27 November. On the following Sunday fortnight, 12 December, Sir Miles had had a stroke, dying the next day, 13 December.

Further study of the cuttings showed that Sir Miles had attended the inquest on 22 November, and had also been present at the cremation ceremony two days later. The *Courier* stated explicitly that Celia LeWarne's parents had stayed at Edgehill Court for the interment on 27 November. It was surely incredible that Sir Miles would have started drawing up a new will until they had left? The date on the sheet of paper suggested that it had taken him a week to come to a decision about the bequest to Corbury, before contacting Gerald Stanton to act for him.

But would Stanton have consented to act, in view of the fact that his wife was, in the last resort, the chief beneficiary under the will? Some solicitors would decline. Suppose, for the purposes of argument, that he did consent, wasn't it astonishing that Sir Miles had changed his mind on a matter so carefully thought out almost at a moment's notice? Because the drafting of the will in correct legal phraseology must have been put in hand early in the week before his death for it to have received his signature at all: he died on 13 December, having had a stroke the day before. Weren't there grounds here for suggesting that Stanton had exercised undue influence? Grounds strong enough to warrant representations in the appropriate quarter?

In mounting excitement Bernard Lister decided to visit Somerset House and find out whether Gerald Stanton had drawn up the will or not. In the meantime the sheet of notes which had so miraculously come into his hands must be most carefully preserved. After some thought he replaced it, together with his notes, between the pages of *Framley Parsonage* where he had found it, covered the book with brown paper, inscribed a fictitious title, which appealed to him, on the spine, and put it among miscellaneous volumes on a different shelf from its fellows. He did not stop to ask who was likely to be on its track: even the remote prospect of being able to dispossess Shirley Stanton had produced in him an excitement bordering on fantasy.

The prospect of waiting until the end of term to verify his facts was intolerable. In spite of pressure of work he managed to fit in a lightning dash to London. For the usual fee a copy of Sir Miles LeWarne's will was made available for his inspection. Within moments he knew that Stanton and Mundy of Corbury had drawn it up, and that it had not been signed until the actual day of Sir Miles's death, Monday, 13 December. Indignation at pressure having been put on a dying man briefly eclipsed his grim satisfaction at this further indication of Gerald Stanton's unprofessional conduct. Then, pulling himself together, he checked the provisions of the will with those in the notes which he had found. They were identical, apart from the cash legacy to Shirley Stanton, and her inheritance of the residuary estate.

Bernard Lister had a vivid imagination, fostered by his lonely childhood. During his return train journey he pictured the signing of the will. Perhaps Sir Miles had struggled to speak, wanting at the last to repudiate the change made against his better judgment. Or perhaps he had been too far gone to remember what he had agreed to, and hadn't really known what he was signing. . . .

It was at this point in his musings that the possibility of a faked will having been presented to Sir Miles for signature suddenly occurred to Bernard Lister. He leant back in the corner of the compartment, holding his breath.

In due course he arrived home, and walked upstairs to his flat like a man in a dream, pausing at the door to select a latchkey from the bunch on his key-ring. Realization that someone was behind him, at the foot of the stairs to the second-floor flat, came a split second too late for evasive action. He was gripped and his arms pinioned, to the accompaniment of a stream of abuse. Struggling vainly he shouted for help, hoping desperately that James Halton was in the house. His assailant, bigger and stronger than himself by far, shook him savagely and swung him round. In a nightmare horror he found the contorted face of Mark Plowman within inches of his own. From the depths of his subconscious the past came surging up, and he cringed involuntarily, shouting in panic.

"You bloody little rat," Mark Plowman snarled, "putting the police on to my little girl!"

As he was flung across the landing to crash into the wall, Bernard Lister suddenly realized why the girl's face which had teased his memory had seemed familiar. In the same instant a door burst open on the floor below. Feet pounded up the stairs, and James Halton hurled himself upon Mark Plowman.

"What the hell goes on?" he demanded. "I saw this bastard assaulting you, Lister. Dial 999, and I'll hang on to him till the police get here. Shut up, you," he added, aiming a kick at his captive's shin.

Bernard Lister automatically straightened his collar and tie. Rescue had dispelled terror: against the towering bulk of James Halton, Mark Plowman was cut down to size.

"He's some chap who thinks I put the police on to the

pot-smoking lot upstairs," he replied. "Apparently his daughter was one of them. No, I don't want to charge him. One can't help being sorry for people whose kids go off the rails," he added, with exquisite malice.

"You filthy little liar . . ." Mark Plowman began furiously. James Halton punched him.

"If you want to know who gave the police a tip-off, I did. Care to take me on? No? Sensible man. Always go for a chap smaller than you are. That's—what—I'm—doing—right—now. And get out! I don't advise a return visit."

As the front door of the house slammed he turned to Bernard Lister.

"Good thing I was still around," he remarked with more truth than tact, indicating various roped and corded packages in the hall below. "As you know, we're off on Sunday. You ought to take up judo, Lister. Weight isn't everything by a long chalk. Come down and have a drink—you look as though you could do with one."

"Thanks, I will. I'm damn' grateful to you, Halton, I need hardly say."

"Don't thank me, old chap. I enjoy a scrap. Come along in, and find yourself a pew. I suppose your caller had been in court," James Halton went on, pouring out a couple of generous whiskies. "The pot case came on today, and the Bench took a pretty tough view of it all. Tresillian was fined a hundred and fifty for letting the flat be used, and the type who supplied the stuff's been jailed. He had LSD on him, too. It's all in the evening rag—take it along, and read it."

As soon as he decently could, Bernard Lister extricated himself. Skimming through the newspaper report, he saw that Belinda Plowman and the two other girls involved had been severely cautioned and discharged. He was relieved that there was no mention of himself as a fellow tenant of David Tresillian's. He reflected with satisfaction that on balance the day had been a good deal more humiliating for Mark Plowman than for himself. For a brief moment the terror of the encounter on the stairs sent a shudder through him, but he was able to push it aside: a very promising prospect had opened up before him.

On regaining his car, Mark Plowman had started off on the road to Corbury, driving so recklessly in his raging fury that he narrowly avoided several crashes. Presently, however, it was borne in on him that the last straw would be if the family found out about his humiliation in front of Bernard Lister. He slowed down automatically. He must stop off somewhere for a wash and brush up, and have something to eat: steady himself down. If he were late enough getting home, Monica might have gone to bed and be asleep. Fortunately he had rung her when they came out of court.

The outcome of this step was that the shameful memory of the immediate past became a little less intolerable. And over a steak, his slow but tenacious mind began to mull over retaliatory action. . . .

No one was more relieved than Shirley Stanton at the outcome of Belinda's appearance in court. On the following morning she paid an early visit to her brother's house to hear the details of his visit to Warhampton, and was subtly complimentary on the line he had taken, disregarding the fact that it had been at her prompting. After a time, feeling that the subject had been adequately ventilated, she turned the conversation to the forthcoming conference of the British Ceramics Manufacturers' Association.

"14 December, isn't it?" she asked. "I'm so glad you've decided to go up for it."

"Yes," Mark replied. "14 December. Let's hope it won't be the usual waste of time."

Shortly afterwards Shirley went off, thankful to be able to give her undivided attention to her own affairs. She was immersed in the alterations at Edgehill Court, and the general planning of her new home, thriving in the interest and hard work, and thoroughly enjoying her enhanced status.

Gerald Stanton also had a good deal on hand. Amid the preoccupations of dealing with Sir Miles LeWarne's estate, and selling his own house in Edge Crescent, the uncomfortable awareness of the fraudulent step he had taken began to fade away. Once or twice, when it briefly returned, he had almost to make an effort to realize that such a thing had ever happened. The present was so full and so rewarding. Like his wife, he sensed an increased personal importance, a most agreeable development, both professionally and socially.

By late November the redecoration of the big drawing room at Edgehill Court was finished to their complete satisfaction. As they stood admiring it, Gerald suddenly remembered his mental picture of a party there on a grand scale and told Shirley about it.

"Come to that, I've had the idea of a really slap-up housewarming party at the back of my mind for some time," she answered. "The right move, don't you think? Say the end of February. Barring accidents, we ought to be in and pretty well straight by then. And I've had another great thought, by the way. How about the Caribbean afterwards? We'll have earned a break, heaven knows."

Gerald thought quickly.

"Yes, I think I could fix up with Mundy to be away from the office then. The Caribbean . . . didn't Lady Ilmington— the Dowager, I mean—say the young ones had stayed at a very decent place in the Bahamas last winter? That time when we were introduced at the point-to-point?"

"Yes, she did. I thought I might contact her."

"Quite," he replied. They exchanged a quick glance of complete understanding.

The following days were particularly busy and satisfactory for him. One, Edge Crescent, sold at a price high even on current inflationary standards. Two new clients of substance presented themselves. The Borough Council had a meeting with some tricky items on the agenda, all of which was disposed of in accordance with the wishes of the inner ring, which included himself. By four o'clock on Friday afternoon, he felt justified in leaving the office early, and was on the point of buzzing for his letters to be brought in for signature when his secretary appeared in person, looking slightly flustered.

"There's a Mr. Spinner in the outer office, Mr. Stanton, who says he must see you urgently. I've told him you don't see clients without an appointment, and suggested he make one for Monday as it isn't your Saturday on, but I just can't get rid of him. Mr. Mundy could fit him in tomorrow morning, but he says he must see you personally and that he's come a long way. I'm very sorry, Mr. Stanton."

Gerald swore briefly.

"What sort of chap is he?"

"He's about your age, Mr. Stanton. He's quite prosperous, I should think, and speaks like an educated sort of person— you know."

"I suppose I'd better see him. Tell him I can only give him

ten minutes, and come in with the letters and remind me I'm
due at a Council meeting at half-past."

"Yes, Mr. Stanton."

She vanished. Trying to smother his annoyance, Gerald
waited. There were footsteps outside, and the door reopened.

"Mr. Spinner to see you, Mr. Stanton," she announced.

Gerald stood up, prepared to be cut and dried. The door
closed behind a short man with dark hair brushed up on end.
He wore an overcoat and white muffler, and a massive pair of
horn-rimmed spectacles. Slowly and deliberately he removed
the latter, and stared fixedly.

"Good God, it's Blister!" Gerald exclaimed, aware of being
inexplicably alerted in the very moment of recognition. "It
must be quite twenty years since we met last. Why on earth
are you calling yourself Spinner? Sit down, man."

Bernard Lister sat down.

"It's a name that has a special appeal for me, as it happens.
A better one than Blister, don't you think? Naturally I thought
you would refuse to see me if I sent in my own name."

Searching for the best line to take, Gerald Stanton seized
on this opening.

"My dear chap," he protested, "your walking out on the
old Plowmans is prehistory. I should have done exactly the
same in your place. At this distance of time one can see what
a raw deal you had."

He saw that he was on the right tack. Blister had not
expected friendliness and was momentarily taken aback.

"I suppose you know Shirley married me?"

Bernard Lister nodded.

"It's in connection with your wife that I've come to see
you."

Gerald Stanton went cold: that instant foreboding had been
fully justified.

"In connection with Shirley?" he queried, with just the
right note of bewilderment.

"Yes. I am in a position to prove that undue influence was
exercised to persuade Sir Miles LeWarne to leave her Edgehill
Court and the rest of his residuary estate. If, indeed, he
actually made the bequest."

By now prepared for this frontal attack, Gerald Stanton was
able to react with convincing incomprehension.

"What the hell are you talking about? I'm simply not with
you."

Tense, Bernard Lister moistened his lips.

"You can cut out putting on an act. I tell you I've written evidence that up to a week before he died Sir Miles intended leaving the Court and the residuary estate to Corbury."

As he spoke he realized with discomfort that his accent had coarsened, oddly reverting to that of his early childhood, and also that Gerald Stanton was aware of it. The two men stared at each other, united in remembered experience, and to Bernard's disadvantage.

"It's possible evidence that Sir Miles considered doing so may have come into your hands," Gerald replied coolly. "He certainly—yes, Miss Fletcher?"

"Your letters for signature, Mr. Stanton. And you remember you are due at a Council meeting at half-past four?"

"Yes, I do. Thanks."

He took a folder from her, glanced at his watch, and turned again to Bernard Lister, steadied by the brief interlude.

"Now, let's get this straight," he said, authoritatively but without heat. "What you have got hold of, I can't imagine, but the facts are these. Sir Miles deliberated at length about whether to make Corbury or Shirley his residuary legatee, in default of a LeWarne to inherit, after his great-nephew had met with a fatal car accident. He finally informed me that he had decided on Shirley. I thought things over, and put it to him that I should much prefer another solicitor to draw up his will if Shirley was to be the chief beneficiary. He refused even to consider this, and got very steamed up, so in view of his age and the appalling shock he had just had over Roger's death, I gave in."

Bernard Lister listened with mounting unease, struggling to free himself from memories of his wretched adolescence among the assured young men and girls of the Plowman set. This interview was not developing along the lines sketched out by his gloating imagination. He made the mistake of shifting his ground.

"If you think I'm going to swallow all this guff, you're vastly mistaken," he said thickly. "There wasn't the time for all you say happened. How about Sir Miles signing this so-called will the very day he died? If that doesn't stink to heaven, I don't know what does."

There was a pause.

"Sir Miles LeWarne," Gerald Stanton said coolly, "signed his will with the full approval of his doctor, who was present in a professional capacity. Two official witnesses were also present, of course."

There was a further pause, during which Bernard Lister struggled to find a vantage point from which to renew the attack. Before he could do so, Gerald Stanton came in again.

"Look here, Bernard," he said in a different tone, avoiding the offensive nickname, "I perfectly understand that you hate the Plowmans' guts, and would go to any length to do them down. Also that this goes for me, too, as I've married Shirley. We were perfectly bloody to you when we were all youngsters, and for what it's worth at this distance of time, I apologize on my own account. Now you imagine that you're on to something that would ruin Shirley and myself for life. Well, I can only assure you that you're mistaken. The suggestions you've been making are ludicrous, not to say actionable. I've already gone a long way further than most solicitors would in giving you information, and because of past history I'm prepared to go further still and show you the letter I finally wrote to Sir Miles agreeing to act for him. I'm assuming that a man of your standing has moral integrity in relation to established facts. I can't go into the matter here and now, because of this Council meeting. But as it happens I have to be in Warhampton on 14 December for a client's case in the Crown Court. I suggest that we meet there. Presumably I can contact you by telephone to fix details? I shall assume that you are prepared to reciprocate with your own written evidence, as you describe it?"

Wholly unconvinced, but aware of having been outmanoeuvred, Bernard Lister attempted to retain his dignity by appearing to deliberate.

"Very well," he said at last. "I'll agree to that. But I warn you that unless I'm completely satisfied, I shall be taking the matter further. . . . I can see myself out."

As his footsteps died away, Gerald Stanton sat on at his desk, cold from shock, and with his thoughts racing. There could be no possible doubt that in some incredible way notes of Sir Miles's real intentions had come into Blister's possession. Not that it mattered how . . . unless, of course, somebody else was involved, who had passed on the information. . . .

Burying his face in his hands, Gerald forced himself to concentrate on essentials. Whoever knew, the urgent thing was the fabrication of the letter which he had told Lister he had written to Sir Miles. It must be carefully drafted, with

clear reference to Shirley's inheritance. Of course, putting
something new into the LeWarne file at this stage was a risk.
Miss Fletcher had referred to its contents for him on several
occasions. However, the risk had to be taken, in case that
swine Blister tried to stir up mud without waiting for the
meeting on 14 December.

With an effort Gerald roused himself to deal with the
contents of the folder which Miss Fletcher had brought in,
signing his letters mechanically without reading them through.
It was vital to carry on normally. Snatching up some papers,
he went to his partner's room and discussed a client's affairs
for a few minutes. The conversation moved on easily to the
weekend's golf prospects, and John Mundy's new car. Finally
Gerald remarked that it had been one hell of a week, and he
was pushing off.

On returning to his own room he found Miss Fletcher
replenishing his stock of the firm's stationery, and commented
casually on the quality of the new batch as he collected some
to take home.

"You were most convincing about the Council meeting,"
he told her. "I soon shot off the chap: a definite nut case with
a persecution complex. I urged him to see a London solicitor:
so much more experienced in handling a difficult case like
this than a poor country bloke."

Miss Fletcher was discreetly amused. Wishing her a good
weekend, Gerald Stanton went downstairs, humming a few
bars of a current pop hit, and greeting the receptionist as he
passed her desk. As he walked to his car, he realized that he
was cold and feeling slightly sick. He drove himself home,
turning down the lane by the side of his house to the garage.
Shirley, he knew, was out and would not be back until supper
time. He switched off the engine and sat on in the car, deliberately assessing the danger of his situation.

It was unquestionably acute. Blister was basically crude
and naïve, but anything but a fool in some ways. Even if he
was forced to withdraw his allegations by convincingly faked
evidence, what guarantee was there that the written evidence
he so inexplicably possessed would be destroyed? Even
if—most probably—he agreed to hand it over, he could easily
have a photostat copy made. And he'd know perfectly well
how easily he could start up damaging rumours, even if they
couldn't be substantiated. A solicitor was as vulnerable as a
doctor to this sort of thing . . .

Shivering now, and dangerously near panic, Gerald pulled himself together with all the strength he could summon up. He must take immediate practical steps. Start on that letter at once—not sit around like this. He got out of his car, locked it, and emerged from the garage. Preoccupied though he was, he was startled to find himself in a world bathed in lurid crimson, and walked the few steps to the gate leading into the excavations. The sunset sky was ablaze almost to the zenith, while to the east a full moon of unnatural size mounted relentlessly. In the foreground loomed ragged mounds and ridges of debris, and partly infilled trial trenches gaped suggestively.

As he contemplated this eschatological scene, an appalling idea flashed across his mind . . . there was only one real solution to a problem like his. . . .

Sweating, he struggled to push the thought from him.

# Part Two

# Chapter 5

The staff of Warhampton University's history department began assembling unenthusiastically for their pre-term meeting on the afternoon of 9 January. Outside, the day was raw and still. Inside, the central heating was potent, and the general atmosphere one of Christmas and New Year hangover, and colds in the head. Small groups stood conversing desultorily while individuals sat aloof, catching up on the weeklies to which they were addicted. Professor Cranford greeted arrivals conscientiously, trying not to be repetitive. He was a short, thick-set man with a massive brow, an acknowledged authority on the Younger Pitt.

By 2:25 the absence of Bernard Lister was beginning to arouse comment. Finally the minute hand of the electric clock on the wall leapt spasmodically to the half hour. The Professor, with an eye on the door, went on with a conversation about double glazing, aware that impatience was building up. At 2:35 he broke off the discussion and went to his desk. There was a general shuffle as people reorientated themselves.

"Uncharacteristic of Lister to be late," he remarked as he sat down. "No doubt he's snarled up in the traffic. It's getting progressively worse in face of the City Council's masterly inactivity. We'd better make a start on matters which don't involve him directly."

There was seldom much on the agenda for this particular meeting, and all such items were soon disposed of. The Professor buzzed his secretary, and instructed her to ring Bernard Lister's flat. Five minutes later she reported that she had been unable to get an answer.

"Well, we can't hold things up indefinitely," Professor Cranford commented. "We must make provisional decisions about these students who want to change their programmes, and anybody Lister feels really strongly about will have to be reconsidered, if necessary. None of you knows anything about his vacation activities, I suppose?"

As he expected, no information on this subject was forthcoming.

Full term began on the following morning. At eleven o'clock a pugnacious Second Year accosted her tutor, Dr. Marcella Wright, the Senior Reader.

"Is Mr. Lister ill, Dr. Wright?" she demanded. "He never turned up for our lecture, and there was no message. And dozens of people have been trying to see him all morning. There's no notice on his door."

Marcella Wright surfaced from hectic activity to realize that she had completely forgotten about Bernard Lister's non-appearance at the staff meeting. As she promised to make enquiries, she felt a sudden qualm. Suppose he was in his flat, but had had a coronary, or something? She was officially free for the next hour, and being a kindly and rather impulsive person, decided to go round and put her mind at rest on this matter at least. After looking up the address she set off in her car.

She did not expect an answer when she rang Bernard Lister's bell, but it was disconcerting to get none from the other two flats. She stared at the front of the house. The only open window was one in Bernard Lister's flat. Otherwise the whole place looked shut up. An attempt to get round to the back of the building was baulked by a locked garden door. There was nothing for it but a return to the University. In transit she made up her mind to report her visit to Professor Cranford.

After listening to her, he admitted to a growing concern of his own.

"It's so utterly out of character for Lister not to have contacted us. Even if he's unconscious in hospital somewhere, he must have had papers of some sort on him, and surely the authorities would have informed the police here? I agree with you," he went on, "that we ought to make sure he isn't in his flat, especially as there's an open window."

"Will that mean bringing in the police?" Marcella Wright asked in dismay.

"I'm afraid it probably will. I suppose I'd better get on to the Vice-Chancellor."

\*     \*     \*

Initially the undermanned Warhampton police reacted with scepticism to a request to check up on Mr. Bernard Lister's flat. When the address was noted, however, there was an immediate interest. The file of the recent cannabis case was consulted, and Sergeant Flack of the City Constabulary told to get the key of the house from the agent, and have a look round.

On arrival, he rang the bell of each flat in turn, and on getting no replies unlocked the front door and entered the communal entrance hall. Mail addressed to Bernard Lister and Dr. Halton lay on the mat and more was stacked on a table. The hall floor was immaculate, suggesting that no one had walked over it since it was last cleaned. Going upstairs, Sergeant Flack tried the door of the first floor flat. It was locked, and he satisfied himself that the key was not on the inside. Pushing up the flap of the letter box, he sniffed. No sinister odour was detectable, merely a general stuffiness. After a rapid inspection of the stairs leading up to the top floor, he threw open the staircase window. As he expected, there was an external iron fire escape which linked all three flats with the back garden. The end wall of this garden abutted on to the grounds of a house shrouded in scaffolding, where men were at work. Within a quarter of an hour he had borrowed a ladder from them, got over the wall, and was standing at the foot of the fire escape.

The short winter afternoon was closing in, but as he looked at what was obviously the bathroom window of Bernard Lister's flat, his attention was alerted. A few seconds later he was examining it at close range, to find that it had been broken near the catch. He decided that any reasonably able-bodied chap could have got on to the sill from the fire escape, but before doing so himself he tried the back door of the flat. He found that it was unlocked, and walked into a small neat kitchen.

"Anyone at home?" he called loudly.

His voice died away into the silence of an empty house, and he proceeded to the bathroom next door. Here there were unmistakable signs of a break-in. A small bedroom, also at the back of the house, contained no feature of interest, and he crossed the landing to the two front rooms. The bedroom contained a single bed, made up but not slept in. Nothing seemed to have been disturbed, and after glancing under the bed and into the cupboards he moved on again.

The door of the adjoining room was ajar. He pushed it open, and the beam of his torch picked out so bizarre a scene that he quickly wrapped a handkerchief round his hand and switched on the light.

The floor and much of the furniture were strewn with fragments of white paper. Stooping to look, Sergeant Flack recognized both typescript and lined paper with handwriting on it. A portable typewriter had been flung across the room, and was lying upside down in a corner. Empty bookshelves lined the walls, their former contents in jumbled heaps on the floor. The drawers of a kneehole desk had been emptied out on to the top. Surprisingly, though, various valuable and easily portable objects, such as a transistor radio and a travelling clock, had not been taken.

Without hesitation he retrieved the desk telephone from the carpet, found that it was live, and dialled his headquarters. While waiting for further instructions he eyed the chaos speculatively. Finally a quack in his ear was followed by a curt order to stay where he was till Inspector Worrall turned up.

A few minutes later there was a ring at the front door bell. He went down to answer it, and found on the doorstep a young man in a burberry, with the expression of a fox terrier on a scent.

"Evening, Sarge. Anything in this for us? *Warhampton Evening News*."

"Not unless you think folks'll be interested in one more small-scale break-in," Sergeant Flack replied. "I suppose one o' those builder chaps tipped you off? Haven't wasted much time, have—"

He broke off as a police car drew up at the kerb. Inspector Worrall got out and strode forward.

"No comment till I've seen the job for myself," he told the young man tersely. "Ring in later, if you think it's worth the price of a call."

Followed by a detective constable carrying fingerprinting gear, the two police officers went into the house.

Later, when Sergeant Flack had left, Inspector Worrall prowled from room to room in the intervals of watching the fingerprinting in progress. He opened drawers and cupboards, and peered into the almost empty refrigerator. Pulling away the bedspread he unearthed a folded pair of pyjamas, which had been worn. He satisfied himself that nowhere was there

any sign of a struggle. Finally, he sat down on the most
comfortable chair in Bernard Lister's bedroom to sort out his
ideas.

Obviously it was not the ordinary type of break-in for theft.
Nor the usual run of mindless vandalism—the damage was
too selective for that. In his own mind he was convinced that
the students ejected from the flat above were responsible. It
looked as though they had wrongly concluded that the tip-off
about the cannabis smoking had come from Lister, and had
decided to get their own back by mucking up his work. All
right, but it was going to be the devil of a job to pin it on to
them. For one thing, when had it happened? After Lister had
left the place, or he would have reported it. By now the chap
was said to be missing, or at any rate hadn't clocked in for the
beginning of the university term. Could the two things be
connected?

After some consideration, Inspector Worrall thought not. It
was unthinkable that the half-baked lot had murdered Lister,
and successfully disposed of his body. At the same time the
two things added up to an odd business, all the more difficult
to sort out with both the other tenants away. Perhaps there
was a working connection, though, because the date when
Lister left the flat was the point at which enquiries into the
students' movements would have to begin.

He took out his notebook and jotted down various leads.
The man must have friends up at the University who'd know
his holiday plans . . . milkman . . . newsagent . . . cleaner
. . . dates of postmarks on mail downstairs. . . . Having
exhausted his ideas for the moment he returned to the sitting
room, where the detective-constable remarked that it would
take anybody a month of Sundays to do the job properly. He
reported finding the same sets of gloved dabs in the bathroom and on various surfaces in the sitting room. Inspector
Worrall grunted.

"Fair enough," he said. "Fix that broken window as best
you can, and we'll knock off for tonight."

The investigation got under way again on the following
morning. The agent for the flats supplied the name and
address of the woman who cleaned the hall and stairs but she
was of little direct help. She knew the three tenants by sight
but did not work for them personally, and could not remember when she had last seen Mr. Lister. By a rare stroke of

luck, however, her sister-in-law cleaned for him: Mrs. Passmore, of 39 Stokes Place.

When run to earth at a local greengrocer's Mrs. Passmore proved rather slow-witted, but sure of the basic facts relating to her employer. She told Inspector Worrall that she cleaned for Mr. Lister Friday afternoon. Leastways, it was Friday afternoon this year. It had to be when he hadn't no lectures to give up to the university, so as he could let her in. A key? No, she'd never had no key to the flat. He wasn't the sort to hand over a key. That was why she always had to go to clean when he hadn't got no—

Cutting in ruthlessly, Inspector Worrall asked her if she could remember when she had last cleaned the flat. Without the slightest hesitation she said that it had been on Friday, 8 December. She was quite certain about it, as 9 December was her old Mum's birthday, and she'd been anxious to get off in good time to finish decorating the cake.

"You're quite sure you didn't go to work at the flat on Friday, 15 December?" he persisted.

"No, I never, not with Mr. Lister going on holiday. I couldn't've got in, see? He paid me up on 8 December with two weeks in advance, same as he always does when he goes on holiday, whether I works or no. 'Tis a retaining fee, like. Then I always gets a postcard, telling me when to start work again, soon as he gets back."

"And you haven't had one yet?"

"Thassright. Any time now, it'll come."

He asked her if she knew where Mr. Lister was going for his holiday. She shook her head. Never said much, he didn't. Lived too much on his own, shut up with all those books, to her way of thinking. But it must've been before the Friday after—15 December that was, or he'd've wanted her to clean as usual.

After impressing on Mrs. Passmore that she must let the police know at once if a postcard arrived from Mr. Lister, Inspector Worrall returned to police headquarters. Here he found that his subordinates had also covered useful ground. Mr. Lister had cancelled deliveries of milk and newspapers as from 15 December until further notice. His car, an Austin Cambridge, had been located in the lock-up which he rented from his garage. It had been brought in for servicing on 14 December, and a note to Mr. Lister propped up on the steering wheel had not been removed.

It now seemed reasonably well established that Bernard Lister had left his flat on 14 or 15 December, and had not returned since. Inspector Worrall put in a report with a feeling of satisfaction. He now had a starting point for the enquiry into the break-in. It would be somebody else's job to track down Lister.

In the meantime, Chief-Superintendent Norrington, who believed in keeping on good terms with people in a position to make nuisances of themselves, had been in conference with the Vice-Chancellor and Professor Cranford. In default of any known relatives of the missing man, the latter felt it incumbent on them to take the initiative. At the same time they were reluctant to involve the University in possibly quite unnecessary sensational publicity. There could be a reasonable explanation of Mr. Lister's absence, such as a mistake on his part about the date of the opening term. After a lengthy discussion, in the course of which Superintendent Norrington put the police view that the break-in was a separate issue, it was agreed to wait another twenty-four hours before getting out a public appeal for information. In the meantime, Bernard Lister's file in the Academic Registrar's office would be consulted, and the referees he had given when applying for his post discreetly contacted.

This cautious plan, however, was destined to be blown sky-high through the unwitting agency of Mrs. Passmore. In common with the majority of Warhampton's citizens, she knew little and cared less about its University, although she was an avid reader of the local evening paper. While perusing it that same evening, she came upon a paragraph on student affairs which struck her as somehow not quite right. She sat with puckered brow until the penny suddenly dropped. Why, the term had started, and there'd been no postcard from Mr. Lister. She reacted indignantly. Given her the push, had he, without a word after four years, and retaining money owing, too? At this moment her husband walked in with his brother, to be greeted with an angry outburst.

"Hold on, Glad," her brother-in-law broke in with some difficulty. "Where's he live, this bloke you works for, and the copper's bin askin' about?"

She told him.

"Cor!" he exclaimed. "That's where I lent a copper a ladder so he could get into the place. I'm orf!"

"Where to?"

"Phone the *Evenin' News*. I'll stand the both of you a round if they pays out again."

The news broke on the front page of the *Warhampton Evening News* twenty-four hours later, under the heading VANISHED LECTURER'S FLAT RANSACKED. A garbled account of Bernard Lister's academic career and non-appearance at the beginning of term followed, and the paragraph ended with an appeal to his relatives and anyone knowing his present whereabouts to contact the Warhampton Police. On the following morning, Saturday, 13 January, the story was put out by the national dailies with varying degrees of accuracy and sensationalism. Telephone calls, mainly from cranks and hoaxers, began to come in, but soon after ten one from Corbury was felt to be sufficiently genuine to be switched through to Chief Superintendent Norrington.

"Good morning, Mrs. Stanton," he said, introducing himself. "I understand you're a relative of Mr. Bernard Lister?"

"Yes, I am, Superintendent," a clear emphatic voice replied. "I'm Mrs. Shirley Stanton, of 1 Edge Crescent, Corbury. My husband's the Town Clerk here, and a local solicitor. Bernard Lister is my first cousin on his mother's side. But I'm afraid I'm not going to be much help: I haven't seen him for over twenty years."

"That's unfortunate. Have you been out of touch with him all this time?"

"Completely. Perhaps I'd better put you in the picture as briefly as I can."

He listened attentively, appreciative of the caller's ability to make a concise statement.

"You say you have a brother, a Mr. Mark Plowman, living in Corbury?" he said, reviewing what she had told him.

"Yes. He runs the family business: Plowman's Pottery. Actually, I'm speaking from there. I came down to show him the paragraph in *The Times*, and as he's engaged, it seemed sensible to ring you myself at once."

"Quite, Mrs. Stanton. You say that as far as you know, your brother has not been in touch with Mr. Lister either. Are there other relatives who might have been?"

"None that I know of. We never knew any of Bernard's relatives on his father's side. Our own family has dwindled almost to nothing over the years. Apart from myself there is just my brother, his wife, and his daughter Belinda. Belinda is a student at Warhampton College of Art, actually. Her name may ring a bell with you, silly girl."

"Yes, I recognize it. I take it that to the best of your knowledge she is not in contact with Mr. Lister either?"

"I think I can vouch for the fact that she's never met him, although she once told me that she'd been to a public lecture he gave."

"Well, Mrs. Stanton, we shall be sending someone down to take brief statements from your brother and yourself, just for the record. We'll ring you to fix a convenient time, of course. Thank you for getting in touch so quickly."

After replacing the receiver, Superintendent Norrington sat for a few moments reviewing his manpower resources, and thinking about Belinda Plowman. Odd how that girl kept cropping up. Only yesterday Worrall had reported interviewing her in connection with the break-in at Lister's flat. He had satisfied himself that she could not have been involved, but had remarked that she had shown the whites of her eyes a bit. Probably another dose of the police was enough to account for it in a girl with her sort of background. After further consideration Superintendent Norrington decided that Worrall was the obvious chap to interview her about Lister, and why she hadn't come forward as a relative. And if he did that, he might as well run down to Corbury, and tackle the rest of the family. That break-in could wait just for the moment.

Inspector Worrall was indignant at being diverted from his pursuit of David Tresillian and his friends, and in consequence was less than tactful in his approach to Belinda Plowman. She promptly burst into tears, protesting that she just couldn't take any more hounding by the police. Surprised, for she had struck him as quite a cool customer, he managed to calm her down and extract a statement that she had never met Bernard Lister in her life, and hadn't the remotest clue as to where he was. She hadn't come forward to say she was a relative because it didn't mean a thing, and would have involved her with the police again.

Fearing a fresh outburst of tears he did not prolong the interview. The next day he drove down to Corbury, in rather better temper. It was sunny and almost spring-like, and he decided that there were worse ways of spending a Sunday on duty. He interviewed Mark Plowman and Shirley Stanton in their respective homes, Shirley apologizing for the pre-move condition of hers. He did not greatly take to either of them. Under Mark's bluffness he thought he detected a tendency to truculence, while Shirley was obviously a rather hard, competent type. Both were friendly and cooperative, however, and their statements were in complete agreement, and also bore out the facts supplied by Superintendent Thomas of the Corbury Constabulary.

"Young Lister was never much of a fit in the Plowman set-up," the latter said. "It was class, for one thing. His Dad had been shovver to old Mrs. P.'s mother and father, you see. Then he had a lot more brains than his cousins, and his aunt and uncle didn't take kindly to that. Mind you, all three kids went to the Grammar School, and were treated the same on the face of it, but for all that Bernard always looked the odd man out, somehow. My, there was the hell of a dust-up when he came into money and cut loose! I can still call it to mind."

"I get you," Worrall said. "Mr. Mark Plowman didn't exactly strike me as the Brain of Britain."

"He certainly hasn't got his old man's business sense," Superintendent Thomas agreed. "It was plain enough the Pottery wasn't doing well, a year or two back. Stuck in a rut. Then Mrs. Stanton came into a pot of money from her godfather—some families have all the luck, don't they?—and gave the place a shot in the arm. Up-to-date kilns, and whatever. It seems to be making out now, from what people say."

This piece of information struck Worrall as being the only potentially useful outcome of his trip to Corbury, but as a lead it quickly petered out. Bernard Lister's solicitor was persuaded to disclose the fact that his client had left no personal or family bequests in his will.

The search for the missing man was intensified and extended. As no recognizable photograph of him appeared to exist, a detailed description was drawn up and circulated. A search of his flat brought his passport to light, suggesting that he had not, at any rate, left the country. Contacts discovered from letters and the stubs of old cheque books were followed up without result. Intensive questioning of his colleagues produced a list of libraries and other places which he was known to visit in connection with his work, but none of these had any record of his presence since the previous November. Under pressure his bank manager revealed that he had cashed a cheque made out to Self on 11 December, but none since. There had been no unusual developments in his personal affairs such as the sale of investments.

In the meantime Inspector Worrall's investigations into the break-in failed to provide any helpful information. After leaving the flat belonging to his aunt, David Tresillian and the students who had been living there with him appeared to have been taken in temporarily by their friends, moving casually from one address to another until they left Warhampton shortly before Christmas. They had all been located and questioned, but maintained a flat denial of having broken into Bernard Lister's flat. Inspector Worrall was convinced that David Tresillian, at least, was lying, but in view of the impossibility of establishing his movements during the period in question after so long an interval, it was decided to suspend the enquiry.

In short, the file relating to Bernard Lister's disappearance achieved a formidable bulk, but he himself had apparently vanished into thin air. As the weeks succeeded each other the enquiry inevitably lost momentum. In accordance with official policy where missing persons are concerned, his file was not closed. It would remain open until the mystery of what had become of him was solved, or his possible life span had come to an end. By the middle of March, however, it could fairly be said to have been shelved for the time being.

# Chapter 6

On 3 June, happily a Sunday, Horace Rudd was to celebrate his half century, and a family reunion was planned. His son Jim and daughter-in-law Eileen arrived on the Saturday with their two children, and were staying in the house. Horace and Winnie Rudd were both natives of Corbury, and a reckless number of local relatives had been invited to join in the birthday festivities. Winnie, who had been cooking ahead for most of the past week, would have been glad of a nice lie-in on the Sunday morning, but her grandchildren's youth and high spirits ruled this out. From an early hour Clive, aged eight, and Linda, six, were pounding up and down the stairs, reporting to Horace on the parcels by his plate and being generally obstreperous. Horace himself was the last down for breakfast, to be greeted by a prearranged yell of "Fifty, not out!" from the younger generation.

Winnie had stipulated in advance that no presents should be opened until breakfast was over.

"Never get the meal finished else," she had insisted. "Don't forget it's hot dinner for fourteen to get going."

The children, who knew what was inside the elongated package labelled "All the best, Dad, from your loving son Jim," became more and more excited as the meal progressed.

"I bet Grandpa'll think it's the most super best present he's ever had," Clive proclaimed. His sister began to bounce up and down in her chair and growl and squeak.

"That'll DO!" their father shouted. "Pipe down, else you won't see him open his presents. It'll be out the back with the pair of you."

More astutely, their mother pointed out that if they didn't hurry up over their food, Grandpa'd be kept waiting to see what he'd got. Recognizing the truth of this statement, they fell to, and soon announced that they were full.

Horace, realizing that any other present would obviously fall flat after his son's, tactfully announced that he'd keep the funny-looking parcel till last. Socks, a pullover, slippers, tobacco and various other gifts were unwrapped in an atmosphere of mounting expectancy. At last, in a breathless hush, he picked up the long thin parcel, weighed it in his hand, shook his head with a mystified expression, and began to remove the outer layer of brown paper. An inner layer of corrugated cardboard came away, and he held a curious object in his hand. It consisted of a thin metal shaft about four feet long, with a battery at one end controlled by a switch. At the other end the shaft expanded horizontally into a not-quite-closed circle, of about six inches in diameter. Horace sat staring at this object, oblivious of a loud hiccup from Linda, followed by a nervous giggle synchronizing with her mother's rebuke. He suddenly looked up at Jim, awed rapture in his face.

"Blimey, it's one o' those metal detectors," he said.

"Got it in one, Dad!" Jim Rudd slapped the table triumphantly. "I picked it up second-hand, but it works a fair treat, don't it, kids? What price Roman coins now? See you in the *Courier* again soon, won't we? Come on, let's have a bash right away."

Various metal objects were put under mats, and the current switched on. The detector functioned perfectly, cutting out its steady hum as the circle was moved over small amounts of metal, and uttering high-pitched yelps as a large iron shovel was approached. The two men and the children were absorbed. Winnie Rudd and her daughter-in-law exchanged humorous pitying glances and began to clear away the breakfast things.

Later, Horace agreed to let Jim run him up to the dig, to have a go on the site. On the way he expatiated on the iniquity of ignorant people who used metal detectors to hunt for buried treasure on archaeological sites.

"So I can't start digging all over the place," he explained. "Might muck things up. We'll try our luck in the part the Archaeological's written off now."

On arriving at the church they had difficulty in parking. The available space was packed with cars, and from inside St. Gundryth's there came a muffled psalm chant.

"The Church Council'll be glad to get the rest of the site levelled and asphalted," Horace went on, as they made their way across the broken ground beyond the Roman villa. "Work's starting this coming week. It should make room for twenty to thirty more cars, I reckon. Only a Trust the Motorist collecting box for the parking fee, same as outside the church, but they say it brings in more than you'd expect."

"How do you digging blokes know for sure there's no more Roman stuff under this part, Dad?" Jim asked.

"See all these trenches?" Horace asked, with a wave of his hand, flattered at his personal inclusion as an authority. "They go down deep as the foundations back there, see? We didn't strike nothing, beyond a few bits of broken pottery. So Mr. Hosford— he's in charge—said we'd call it a day."

"Left the place in a bit of a mess, haven't you?" Jim commented, looking about it.

"Archaeological's paying to have the infilling done proper. Mr. Hosford said it was better to push on with the villa."

"What about a go just here?"

The metal detector immediately located a large rusty nail in the rubble. They moved on, and unearthed a metal staple, and a small unidentifiable piece of iron. Finally, a triumphant Horace Rudd straightened himself up with a horseshoe in his hand.

"Here, we'd better be getting back," he said, looking across to the clock in the church tower. "There's company to dinner, and Mother won't be best pleased if they start turning up and us still out."

Jim, now thoroughly bitten with treasure-hunting fever, was reluctant to give up.

"Let's have one more go, Dad. This trench here, with all this loose stuff chucked in."

Apart from themselves the site was deserted. They were now out of range of the church service. The June sun beat down on them from a cloudless sky, and the only sound was the purr of the metal detector as Horace guided it over the partly infilled trench. He started as it abruptly emitted a loud high-pitched note.

"Something under here all right," Jim exclaimed. "Gimme the trowel."

Bending down he worked energetically, throwing out scoops of rubble. About eighteen inches down he struck a hard object. Almost immediately they both noticed the unpleasant smell. For Horace it instantly resuscitated wartime experiences long and mercifully forgotten. Before he could speak,

Jim had succeeded in levering up a sheet of corrugated iron. With a strangled gasp he let it fall back again.

They stood and stared at each other in speechless horror. Horace, who had encountered similar sights before, was the first to recover his powers of speech.

"God Almighty!" he said hoarsely. "It's a police job, this. There's a call box at the top o' High Street. You best stay here, Jim."

"So as soon as the Allchester CID got the chap identified by a dentist as the missing lecturer from Warhampton, the two Forces saw they'd be getting under each other's feet, and their C.C.s agreed to pass the buck to us," concluded Detective-Superintendent Tom Pollard of New Scotland Yard. "And here we go."

Although the big black Hillman was touching ninety on the M4, Detective-Inspector Toye at the wheel had been missing nothing of his Chief's résumé of the case. Regretfully he began to reduce speed and get out of the fast lane.

"Then the last person known to have seen Lister was this garage hand?" he asked, as the speedometer needle settled at seventy.

"This is it. A young chap who swears that he saw Lister bring in his car in the early afternoon of 14 December, and put it into the lock-up he rents from them. He'd already arranged for the car to be serviced the next day, or as soon as they could get it done while he was away."

Toye reflected further.

"What do you make of the state of Lister's flat, sir?" he enquired. "I don't mean the break-in, but milk left in the fridge, and all the usual toilet articles in the bathroom, and whatever."

"It looks to me as though Lister went off—voluntarily or otherwise—later on 14 December. He may of course have only meant to be away for a night or two in the first instance, and just taken a toothbrush and a comb. That would tie up with the bed's being left made up, and the soiled pyjamas. For lack of anything more definite at the moment I'm prepared to work on the assumption that zero-hour was the 14th."

"Seems to me," Toye said, "that the Warhampton chaps threw their hand in too soon over that break-in. If it could be proved to have been on the night of 14 December, Lister must have gone by then, and never came back."

"Yes," Pollard agreed. "I can't see anything for it but reopening the break-in enquiry. I agree with Warhampton that those students stick out a mile. And to my mind there's an end-of-term touch about the business: a sort of rag gone rotten. The university term ended on the morning of 14 December."

They had left London early, and by noon were closeted with Superintendent Thomas of the Corbury Constabulary.

"We wanted a natter with you, Super, before the other chaps turn up," Pollard told him. "You're our man on Lister's home ground, and you can fill us in as nobody else can."

Superintendent Thomas, not a little overwhelmed by recent events in Corbury, warmed to this approach.

"Nice of you to put it that way, Mr. Pollard," he said. "Though mind you, it's my opinion that Lister's being who he was hadn't anything to do with his being murdered. There've been some nasty cases of mugging in these parts lately. Thugs coming over from the big towns, of course. Mostly over to Allchester, it's true, but we had one here in Corbury which we've never been able to clear up. An elderly gent beaten up and robbed. In hospital for a fortnight, he was. Now Lister was cleaned right out—watch, wallet, loose cash, keys, everything. I reckon some young thugs hit him a bit too hard, then got scared and had the bright idea of dumping the body in a handy ready-made grave up at the excavations. Plenty of folk know about them. And there's nothing to show the murder happened here in Corbury. The body could've been brought in a car."

"Broad and long, though, the mugging fraternity doesn't run to cars," Pollard observed. "You may be right about Lister's being a chance victim, but all the same I'd like to get him into context, so to speak. I gather he was an orphan, brought up here by an uncle and aunt. Well-to-do local business people, weren't they?"

"That's his background," Superintendent Thomas replied. "Plowman's Pottery's the family business. I daresay you noticed it down at the bottom of the town as you came in. . . ."

He began to talk with the countryman's deliberation, but pithily. Pollard listened attentively, jotting down a note from time to time.

"Thanks a lot, Super," he said, when the narrative came to an end. "Just the sort of thing that's so useful at the start of a case. I'm not a man to write off coincidence," he went on.

"I've run up against it too often. But at first sight the fact that Lister's body has turned up in this place is suggestive to say the least of it. In your opinion can we accept the fact that he never came back here after cutting loose from the Plowmans?"

Superintendent Thomas sat in silence for a moment or two while considering the matter.

"I'll say we can," he came out at last. "It's this way, Mr. Pollard, Corbury's a small place. It's grown a bit lately but there aren't all that many incomers, even now. This part of the world's a bit off the map, too. Why, they didn't give us our postcode till the end of last year. It all throws people in on themselves, if you get me, and makes 'em mighty interested in each other's business. Memories as long as your arm they've got for what's happened to folk in the past, too. If Bernard Lister'd shown his nose in the place, I'd expect somebody to recognize him, even after all this time, and there'd've been talk. And that sort of talk nearly always comes our way in time, seeing one or two of my chaps are Corbury born and bred, and married to local girls."

"About these cousins of Lister's," Pollard pursued after a short pause. "—Mr. Mark Plowman and Mrs. Stanton. As far as I can make out from the file his body was found a stone's throw from their back doors. Do you think it's at all likely, in spite of what they say, that Lister *had* recently been in touch with either or both of them and was on his way to call when he was mugged and killed? And that when they knew what had happened they decided to keep quiet to avoid being caught up in the enquiry?"

Superintendent Thomas gave him a long look.

"I couldn't say such a thing's impossible, Mr. Pollard, but it doesn't ring true to me. The family were wild when he walked out on them. It was a sort of nine days' wonder in the town. Most local feeling was on their side, too. Ingratitude, people said, after they'd given him a home and his schooling and let him go to Oxford instead of into a job right away. And it was thought shameful when he never even came back to the funerals when his uncle and aunt went. No, I just can't see Mr. Mark and Mrs. Stanton having anything to do with him now."

"Lister had money, hadn't he?" Pollard queried.

"That's true. But Mrs. Stanton came in for a packet from her godfather, and a nice place into the bargain. Edgehill

Court, it's called, just outside the town. She and her husband are living there now."

"But how about Mark Plowman? There's something in the file about the Pottery not doing well at one time."

"No more it was, a few years ago. But when Mrs. Stanton came into her money she gave it a shot in the arm. Put in new equipment. It's doing all right now, from the look of things. They've just opened a showroom in High Street, to catch the visitors who came for the Millenary."

"The Millenary?"

"That's right. A thousand years ago this year Corbury got its charter from King Edgar, and the land to build the parish church on. We're having no end of a set-out in August, with Americans coming over from Corbury, U.S.A. Plowman's are getting out souvenirs in a big way."

"Well, well," Pollard said. "Jolly interesting. Wish I could come along myself." He looked at his watch. "We'd better go and get a bite before the inquest, Toye. See you at the pow-wow afterwards, then, Super."

The adjourned inquest on the body found by Horace Rudd and his son was reopened at two o'clock. After Bernard Lister's dentist from Warhampton had given conclusive evidence of identity, it was further adjourned for a month, to enable the police to continue their enquiries. Afterwards a brief meeting took place at the police station, at which the Chief Constables of Allchester and Warhampton formally handed over the investigation to Pollard. They then departed by car, to the accompaniment of clicking Press cameras, including that of the *Corbury Courier*'s photographer.

"Well, this is where we muscle in, I suppose," Pollard said. "First stop, the scene of the crime. Can you let us out by another door, Super, to dodge the newshounds?"

A steep side road brought them out near the church. Pollard stopped to gaze up at St. Gundryth's great tower.

"The worst of a job like ours is that even if you get a case in a decent place, there's no time to look round," he grumbled as they walked on towards the excavations. "Look, there's the Roman villa. Lead thou me on, or I'll be here for hours instead of getting on with the job."

Inspector Toye helpfully pointed out sundry pieces of machinery for use in the extension of the car park outside the church.

"Makes you think, doesn't it?" he said. "If they'd got on

to the job last week, I don't suppose the body would ever have been found."

"I wonder how often it works the other way," Pollard speculated. "The luck on the murderer's side by a hair's breadth, I mean. Here's the trench, optimistically roped off. I expect about a hundredweight of bits of stone has been carried off by ghouls."

Knowing that an exhaustive search of the area had already been made, they went on through the gate leading to the land behind the houses in Edge Crescent. Toye remarked that the lie of the land couldn't be handier for anybody in one of these wanting to dump a stiff on the dig.

"If you kept in close under the end wall of these gardens, you'd be out of sight of the windows," he said. "Number 1 is nearest the gate, but number 4 is no distance along."

Pollard agreed. It struck him how secluded the lane and its garages were, ending beyond the last house. Apart from the chance late return of a resident's car, you could reasonably bank on its being deserted on a December night, for instance.

Toye showed interest in the garages, the doors of several of which had been left open by their owners.

"Nice and dry, for all that they wouldn't have a damp course," he remarked. "Two-car family, Mr. and Mrs. Stanton. That'll be the lady's smart new runabout."

He stood contemplating a shining Austin Mini Clubman.

"Let's make a call at number 4," Pollard said. "Plowman was at the inquest, but went off quickly afterwards. He'll probably be down at his Pottery now, but with any luck his wife will be in. After seeing this set-up and its obvious possibilities, I think the more we know about the Plowmans and Mrs. Stanton, the better."

Monica Plowman came to the door herself. Pollard saw a woman approaching middle age, still pretty in a conventional way, but definitely unsmart. She looked at them enquiringly. He watched her closely as he introduced Toye and himself, but could detect no sign of disquiet.

"I expect you want to see my husband," she said at once. "I'm afraid he's at the Pottery, and I don't expect him home before half past five. Is there a message I could give him?"

Pollard deliberately hesitated, and got the hoped-for invitation to come in. The drawing room into which they were escorted intrigued him. Pre-war, he decided, and wondered if this was due to a shortage of money or innate conservatism.

"I don't want to take up more of your husband's time than I must, Mrs. Plowman," he said, "but as he and Mrs. Stanton seem to be the late Mr. Lister's only surviving relatives, we're hoping that they may be able to help us. Do you think it would be more convenient for him if we went down to the Pottery now, or called back here later?"

This simple question seemed to cause Monica Plowman some anxiety. As he watched her deliberate, Pollard wondered if she were afraid of her husband.

"I—I think, perhaps, it would be better if you went down to see him now," she finally decided, adding unconvincingly that she was not sure of his plans for the evening. "But I'm afraid he's not likely to be of much help. I expect you've been told the whole story of how badly Bernard Lister behaved to Mark's family, and that they've been out of touch ever since?"

Pollard made an encouraging affirmative noise.

"One doesn't want to speak ill of the dead, of course," she went on rather doubtfully, "but the Plowmans felt it very much, after all they'd done for Bernard. He wrote a dreadful letter to Mark's parents, and after that nothing more was ever heard from him. So you see, neither my husband nor my sister-in-law can tell you anything about him."

"It must have been very unpleasant for you all at the time," Pollard commented sympathetically.

"Actually it was before Mark and I met," she told him, "so I wasn't involved personally."

"You didn't know Mr. Lister, then?"

Monica Plowman shook her head.

"No, I've never even seen him."

Having learnt what he had come to find out, Pollard led the conversation on to more general topics, and rose to take his leave, after asking to be directed to the Pottery.

"How did you size her up?" he asked Toye, when they were clear of the house.

"Scared of her husband, but not of us," Toye replied. "But not easy in her mind, somehow. Difficult to put your finger on."

"I think she's puzzled, rather than anything else, and a bit browned off. An easy-going type who probably resents all this business. But if her husband killed Lister, I'm dead certain she knows nothing about it. Here's this showroom Thomas was talking about."

They paused at a shop window in which pottery was displayed, including a number of jugs and beakers bearing a coat of arms, and the dates 973–1973.

"I like those beakers with names on them," Pollard remarked. "Good design and a nice glaze. Let's see if they've got a couple I could take back for the twins."

The little shop was obviously a new venture, freshly decorated and smelling strongly of paint. The saleswoman in charge was fair, fat and forty, and greeted them effusively.

In response to Pollard's enquiry, she darted to a shelf, and began to search among the rows of beakers. One inscribed 'Andrew' was triumphantly produced.

"And your little girl's name is Ro-oo-se," she said, dragging a chair forward, and standing on it. "Such a sweet old-fashioned name . . . Now, let me see . . . Do you know, I'm terribly afraid Rose isn't here at the moment. Heather, yes, several Heathers, but no Rose. But I'll ring the Pottery. Our main stock's down there, you see. No trouble, no trouble at all . . ."

She vanished into a cubicle at the back. Avoiding Toye's eye, Pollard examined a stack of flower vases destined for American visitors to the Millenary celebrations. Under the coat of arms was an inscription "Corbury, England, 973–1973, greets Corbury, U.S.A."

"Yes, they've got Rose for you," the saleswoman carolled, reappearing. "So lucky! It's coming up specially within the hour, if you could just have a look round our dear old town. The church is *very* well worth a visit."

Pollard hurriedly explained that he was on his way to the Pottery, and would collect the second beaker there. He paid for both and managed to escape, followed by Toye. Outside they both inhaled gulps of fresh air and headed for the police station to pick up their car.

The atmosphere at the Pottery was one of production rather than effusive salesmanship. Seeing a door marked ENQUIRIES, Pollard went in, and gave his official card to a typist.

"Would you ask Mr. Plowman if he could spare me a few minutes?" he asked, "And I want to collect a beaker with the name "Rose" on it. Your saleswoman rang down about it just now. It's been paid for at the shop."

The girl gaped at him.

"That's right," she said incoherently. "They're packing it up. I'll take it in."

A minute or so later she reappeared, and led Pollard and

Toye to Mark Plowman's office. A solidly-built fair man with a reddish face and a square jaw got up from behind a desk.

"Good evening," he said briefly. "Sit down, won't you?" He bowed slightly in Toye's direction as Pollard introduced him.

Taking his cue, Pollard cut his preamble to a minimum.

"I don't want to waste your time, Mr. Plowman, so may we take it as read that we've been briefed on the late Mr. Bernard Lister's connection with your family, and the breaking-off of relations while he was an undergraduate at Oxford?"

Mark Plowman leant back in his chair, his hands thrust into his trousers pockets.

"As far as I'm concerned we can," he replied. "Always assuming that you realize the break was entirely his doing."

"Quite. I was about to add this. It is not in dispute. Could you take up the story from there, Mr. Plowman."

"There's no story to take up. That was the end of it. After the way he'd behaved, we naturally didn't make any over-tures, and nothing further was ever heard from him."

"A theory about Mr. Lister's death which we're investigat-ing," Pollard went on after a short pause, "is that he decided to revisit Corbury, and was attacked and fatally injured by muggers, who hit on the excavations as a good place to hide the body. We're trying to find out if anything is known of such a projected visit."

There was a further pause, during which Pollard took stock of the man facing him. Difficult customer, he thought. No imagination. Very set in his ways for a chap of his age, and aggressive into the bargain. Or is it really defensiveness, from an unadmitted knowledge that he hasn't made much of a go of life?

At this point Mark Plowman gave him a hostile glance.

"If you're hinting that Bernard Lister contacted me and suggested a meeting, the answer is an unqualified no. I shouldn't have agreed to it if he had. And I know I can answer for my sister, Mrs. Stanton, too, although I don't suppose you'll accept my word for it."

"There's an established routine in these matters," Pollard replied calmly. "Reverting to Mr. Lister, can you think of anyone at all in the area whom he might have wanted to visit?"

He thought, but was not certain, that Mark Plowman relaxed slightly.

"Afraid I can't. He wrote an abominable letter to my parents at the time, abusing the town and everybody in it, as well as ourselves. The plain fact is, Superintendent, that he was a damned unpleasant little bastard with a warped mind."

Pollard wondered briefly if it had ever occurred to the Plowmans that they had any responsibility for Bernard Lister's outlook on life. He switched his mind back to his last question.

"Mr. Lister was a professional historian," he said. "Is there anyone of that sort living 'round here?"

"No one I've ever heard of. The history master at the Grammar School in our time was pretty good at his job, but he died a few years ago."

"Just one thing more, Mr. Plowman, and then we'll be through. The difficulty in this case is that Mr. Lister seems to have been such a solitary person, both in regard to relatives and friends. Because of this fact, we can only make a start by following up such contacts as he is known to have had, as a matter of routine. As far as we know at present, the last time he was seen alive, except by his murderer, of course, was on 14 December of last year. You won't misunderstand me, I'm sure, if I ask you to make a formal statement of your movements on that date."

Mark Plowman looked ugly, but controlled himself.

"You may say this sort of thing is routine, Superintendent, but it strikes me as personally offensive. However, I suppose you're legally entitled to treat people like this. As it happens, I remember clearly where I was on 14 December: at an important business meeting in London."

A series of exchanges followed, as a result of which it was established that he had gone up to London by the 9:30 a.m. train from Allchester, to a meeting of the British Ceramics Manufacturers in connection with a forthcoming exhibition. The meeting had been held at the Waterbury Hotel in Holborn, and gone on until half-past three. He had then taken a taxi to the Victoria and Albert Museum, to study designs of nineteenth century pottery with a view to introducing some new lines at Corbury, leaving shortly before closing time and being much delayed in getting back to his hotel in Bloomsbury, the Hamilton, by the rush hour traffic. As a result, he had decided to eat out without first returning to the hotel, and had a meal in a steak house somewhere near the Oxford Street end of Tottenham Court Road. He had not noticed its name. He had then dropped into a News Theatre near by for about a couple of hours, and then walked back to the Hamilton. Nothing much seemed to be doing in the bar, so after having a drink he had gone up to bed. On the following morning he had gone down to the City for an appointment with some export agents in Prince Consort Street, and taken a taxi from there to Paddington, for the midday train back to Corbury.

Without comment Pollard asked Toye if he had got everything down, and on getting an affirmative answer thanked Mark Plowman for his co-operation and brought the interview to an end.

"Full of holes as a sieve, between the end of the Ceramics meeting and the nightcap in the hotel bar," he commented as they got into the Hillman. "I wonder what he was really doing? He certainly couldn't have murdered Lister and got the body down to Corbury in the time."

"Bird?" queried Toye.

"Could be. I can imagine that Mrs. Plowman's palled a bit. We'll make a start by getting his programme checked by some poor devils back home. You know, it's a bit late now to go on to Mrs. Stanton before supper. We'll eat first."

They called in at the police station, where Pollard rang the Yard at some length on the subject of Mark Plowman's alibi, and then returned to their hotel. Towards the end of their meal a waitress brought Pollard a visiting card. He studied it, and asked her to tell the gentleman that he would be with him in ten minutes.

"Edmund Catchpole, M.A., F.R.Hist.S., F.S.A.," he read aloud to Toye, "Archivist to the City of Allchester."

Toye blinked behind his horn-rims.

"Looks as though your idea of Lister's coming down here to see somebody in the same shop could be right on the beam, sir."

"Corbury's a good thirty miles from Allchester, and the branch line's been closed. Lister hadn't got his car, remember. Still, I suppose he might have been mugged in Allchester on his way to see this bloke, and the corpse carted over here. But you'd think this Catchpole chap would have come forward if Lister hadn't turned up for an appointment, with all the publicity there's been. Here, finish your coffee and we'll go and see what he's got for us—if anything."

Edmund Catchpole was an elderly man with a neatly

trimmed, small grey beard. He shook hands formally and expressed a hope that Pollard and Toye had finished their dinner.

"I enquired for you at the police station," he said, "and was directed here. I may say that I'm approaching you with considerable diffidence."

"Please don't feel like that, sir," Pollard told him. "At this stage in a homicide enquiry, any piece of information may turn out to be valuable."

Mr. Catchpole looked anxiously round the hotel lounge.

"What I have to say is highly confidential. Perhaps we are rather public here."

Pollard suggested that they should go and sit in the car, wondering what could be coming.

When they were settled, Mr. Catchpole cleared his throat in the manner of one about to deliver a lecture.

"While it may have no relevance to the late Mr. Bernard Lister's untimely death," he began, "as his body was found under such—er—unusual circumstances, I felt that it was my duty to inform the authorities that he had recently achieved a breakthrough in an important piece of historical research relating to Corbury. But perhaps I am telling you what you already know from investigations in his flat at Warhampton?"

"No, sir," Pollard assured him. "Carry on, please."

"You are probably aware," the archivist resumed, "even if this is your first visit to Corbury, that the borough plans to celebrate its alleged Millenary in August. I say alleged, because its claim to have received a charter from King Edgar in the year 973 has been discredited for some time by serious historians. The original document—if it ever existed—has disappeared. In the middle of the fifteenth century, however, a charter embodying its alleged provisions, together with those of subsequent early charters whose originals are also missing, was enrolled—registered, that is—at the Chancery Office and received the Royal Seal. It is now in the Allchester archives. To cut a long story short, Mr. Bernard Lister recently established beyond any reasonable doubt that this document is a forgery perpetrated by the leading citizens of Corbury of that time."

"Super!" Pollard exclaimed, carried away by this absorbing piece of local history.

"I presume you are referring to Mr. Lister's achievement, although I admit that the persons involved showed remarkable enterprise and ingenuity. And the whole affair is an interesting sidelight on administrative conditions during the Wars of the Roses. However, I mustn't digress. I need hardly point out that Mr. Lister's discovery came at a singularly awkward moment for Corbury."

Pollard, who had been listening with keen interest, exchanged a quick look with Toye.

"Awkward is the word," he agreed. "It would have made the Millenary celebrations look silly, and possibly involved local traders in quite considerable commercial loss."

"Exactly," Mr. Catchpole replied reluctantly. "And that, I'm afraid, is just what Mr. Lister was hoping to do. He invited me to lunch with him immediately after his discovery. I—er—did not enjoy the meal, which he treated as a kind of celebration. He ordered champagne and, while in no sense the worse for drink, was uninhibited on his dislike of Corbury, where I gathered he had spent an unhappy childhood. He positively gloated over the disclosure he was now in a position to make. I really felt most uncomfortable."

"Can you remember the date of this lunch?" Pollard asked, suddenly visited by an idea.

"It was on Thursday, 28 September, last year. Mr. Lister had come down to Allchester on the previous Sunday, and been working in the Record Office each day."

There was a short silence, broken by Mr. Catchpole's once again clearing his throat.

"Perhaps you will think that this is a trifling matter to raise during an investigation into a murder," he said, "but whatever Mr. Lister's motives were in researching into the Corbury charters, he should certainly receive posthumous recognition for his work. Can you tell me if anything in writing on the subject has been found in his flat?"

"I can't at the moment," Pollard told him. "I haven't yet been to Warhampton. Inspector Toye and I plan to go there tomorrow. I'll make enquiries as soon as I can, and let you know. But, as I expect you read in the papers, whoever broke into the flat tore up a lot of typescript as part of making hay of the study."

Mr. Catchpole looked appalled.

"I must have missed that. Incomprehensible vandalism, isn't it? I suppose one has to accept that it's a recurrent historical phenomenon."

"Unless the vandals were exceedingly thorough, it should

be possible to do some reconstruction. You could probably suggest someone familiar with that kind of subject?" Pollard asked.

The archivist felt sure that he could, and the interview ended on a more cheerful note, Pollard reiterated his promise to look into the matter and report to Allchester in due course.

"Decent old fellow," he remarked, as they watched an elderly Morris drive off. "What price his nice peaceful job, with office hours? The only documents I'm ever likely to study are case files. We'd better get down to this one, and put off Mrs. Stanton until tomorrow morning. I'll go and ring her for a date."

# Chapter 7

At nine-thirty on the following morning Pollard and Toye arrived at Edgehill Court, to keep an appointment with Shirley Stanton made over the telephone on the previous evening.

"Picture, isn't it?" Toye remarked, as they walked across the gravel sweep to the front door and rang the bell.

Before Pollard could reply the door was opened by a tall, dark man, spruce in appearance and assured in manner.

"Superintendent Pollard? I'm Gerald Stanton, Mrs. Shirley Stanton's husband. Do come in."

"You're a solicitor, and the Town Clerk of Corbury, I think?" Pollard said as they shook hands. "This is Inspector Toye, who is working with me on the case."

Gerald Stanton acknowledged Toye pleasantly.

"I see you've got us all taped," he said with a smile. "My wife's in here."

He led the way into a large room on the left, which Pollard immediately thought one of the most beautiful of its kind that he had ever seen. As they entered, a fair woman with a marked resemblance to her brother got up from a chair.

"Won't you sit down?" she invited, when the Yard men had been introduced.

As they settled themselves Gerald Stanton, perched on the arm of a settee, glanced at his watch.

"Do forgive me," he said. "I know this isn't according to the book when Scotland Yard pay one a visit, but I'm due in court in half-an-hour, and there's something involving myself I'd like to tell you, Superintendent. May I go ahead?"

"By all means," Pollard replied, concealing his surprise.

"It arises out of a phone call from my brother-in-law last night, after you had seen him at the Pottery." Gerald Stanton crossed one foot over the other, and sat with folded arms. "According to him, you people now think that 14 December

may be the operative date in this extraordinary disappearance
of Bernard Lister from Warhampton. Of course, down here
we only see the national papers, and a rehash of the week's
news in our local rag. Perhaps there was fuller reporting in
the Warhampton area. But the impression I, at least, formed
was that the police were working on the theory that he had
gone off on holiday, and vanished while away."

"Looking back on it now," Shirley Stanton said, "I can see
that I rather took that for granted, too. The fact that the
description of Bernard was so widely circulated, and appeals
made for anyone who had seen him anywhere to come forward did suggest it."

"I haven't yet studied the Press coverage at the time,"
Pollard told them, "but from what you say, it sounds as
though your deduction was a perfectly understandable one.
How do you come in, then, Mr. Stanton?"

Gerald Stanton met his eyes and grinned.

"I was in Warhampton for the best part of 14 December
last. Very fully occupied in defending a client in the Crown
Court, but there I was. He was a local chap, up on a dangerous driving charge, George Phillips by name."

"That seems a very convincing reason for your presence.
Did you by any chance encounter Mr. Bernard Lister?"

"I did not. At least, to be strictly accurate, I'm not at all
sure that I should have recognized him if I had, after all this
time. We were in the same age group, to use the current
jargon, but naturally I didn't see as much of him as my wife
and her brother, for example, did. She and I weren't even
engaged when he vamoosed. Shall I fill in a bit, for the
record? It might save time later."

"Please do, Mr. Stanton. It's helpful of you to have let us
know about this now. Sooner or later your being in Warhampton would have come out, and we are following up all the
links with Corbury, of course."

Gerald Stanton clasped his hands behind his head, and
closed his eyes briefly.

"I went up for the day," he said, opening them again. "We
were very busy at the office just then, and it's less disrupting
than being away for the night. Our case was perfectly straightforward, and I got the lowdown on our position on the list.
Warhampton's a hundred and forty miles odd, a bit over
three hours if you're lucky with traffic and weather. I reck-
oned that if I got there by ten I'd be perfectly safe. My wife

nobly gave me breakfast at half-past six, and I left here at seven, and got in at ten past ten. I parked at the Grand Central Hotel—do you know Warhampton, by the way?"

"No," Pollard said. "I'm about to pay my first visit today."

"Well, the hotel's about three minutes' walk from the court, so it seemed the best thing to leave the car there, as Phillips had said he'd book a table for lunch. The case before ours was getting through nicely when I arrived, but it dragged on a bit and we didn't get under way until after twelve. Then there was the break for lunch, and I began to wonder if I might have to stay up overnight. However, we were through by a quarter past four and I managed to see to everything and dash off by half-past. I downed a quick cuppa at the Grand Central and was driving down the main street by five to five. There's a hideous clock tower on an island, so I can be sure of the time. I must own to belting along a bit on the way home, but some friends were coming for the night. My wife says I turned up at five past eight."

"We'd just started dinner," Shirley Stanton said. "I'd spun out drinks as long as I could, but felt I couldn't hold up the meal any longer."

"To round off my statement in the approved style," Gerald Stanton added, "the friends were a Colonel and Mrs. Hayter, from Longstaple."

"A full day," Pollard commented. "Thank you. It's a useful bit of help."

"Having done my duty as a citizen in one capacity, I'd better be off and do it in another, before the local Bench. . . . Superintendent, I do hope this wretched business isn't going to be very protracted. It's decidedly unpleasant for all of us. Of course, we're known locally, and so is the long break with Bernard Lister, but we can't help feeling a bit—well, conspicuous."

"I quite realize that it must be very disagreeable for you indeed," Pollard replied. "I can assure you that the investigation is going ahead with all possible speed."

"I'm sure it will, more especially now I've met you. Good-bye, and all possible good luck."

As the door closed behind her husband, Shirley Stanton suggested coffee. Pollard thanked her, and politely refused, saying that he and Toye must be on the road to Warhampton.

"I needn't keep you long," he said. "It's just a question of a formal statement of how you spent 14 December, say from midday onwards."

"I started thinking back when my brother rang last night," she told him, "and remembered how tiresomely things had worked out, with my husband having to chase up to Warhampton, and visitors arriving for dinner. . . ."

As she talked, Pollard observed her with interest. More brains than Mark, he thought, and much more enterprise. Where he's dug in, so to speak, she's moved with the times and widened her horizons. Thrilled to bits with fetching up here as a grande dame. . . .

". . . Pensioners' Christmas Tea in the Town Hall. It really was most inconvenient with the Hayters arriving—I do all my own cooking, even now—but I felt I simply must go. You see, the LeWarnes, who lived here for centuries, were to all intents and purposes Lords of the Manor of Corbury, and dear old Sir Miles who left me the Court knew that I'd do my best to carry on the family tradition. He was my godfather, you know, and a very old friend of my parents, so I do take this sort of responsibility rather seriously. However, I don't mind admitting that I came away as soon as I felt I could, and got home to put the last touches to the dinner before the Hayters turned up about half-past-five. They're old friends, and have a standing invitation to break their journey here if they're driving down from London or from their married daughter in Suffolk, but really they hit on a most awkward evening. I'd hoped Gerald would be back in good time, but when he hadn't appeared by eight we started on the meal, as I said just now. We had hardly begun when I heard his car at the door. All this was when we were still at Edge Crescent, of course. Then after dinner we had a chatty sort of evening and went up to bed about eleven, as far as I remember. I hope this is the sort of thing you want?"

Pollard assured her that her statement was perfectly adequate.

"Just two more points," he said. "Have you at any time been in touch with Mr. Bernard Lister since he cut himself off from the family?"

Shirley Stanton looked him in the face with complete frankness.

"Never at any time," she replied emphatically. "If he had made any advance he would have got no change whatever out of me. I always disliked him, and feel very strongly about his behaviour to my parents."

"And have you ever heard any rumours of his having revisited Corbury at any time during the past twenty-two years, isn't it?"

"No rumours. Nothing so well-founded, if that makes sense. My niece, Belinda Plowman, once said she thought she'd seen him in High Street, but as they had never met, other than her having once been to a lecture he gave, I frankly didn't take her seriously. To be honest, I thought she was trailing her coat to see how I'd react. My brother is still rather rabid about Bernard, and to her it's all old hat and quite absurd."

"When was this, Mrs. Stanton? Some time ago, or recently?"

"Oh, quite recently. Last summer, when we were still at Edge Crescent. I can't remember exactly when, but it must have been during her vacation. I have an idea it was not long before she went back to college."

"Well, many thanks," Pollard said. "I don't think there are any further points, so Inspector Toye and I had better be getting off: At this time of day I doubt if we'll make quite the time your husband did on the Warhampton run."

"He drives much too fast," she said, as they went out into the hall. "I don't want to be repetitive," she added, pausing at the top of the steps, "but as my husband said just now, this really is being grim for us. The local paper full of our photographs, and the past all raked up. It's so unfair."

Pollard glanced at the angry resentment in her face, accentuated by the patches at her cheekbones.

"I understand how you are feeling," he replied with truth, "but I can only be repetitive myself. We shall do everything possible to investigate Mr. Lister's murder, and bring the person or persons responsible to justice with the absolute minimum of delay. Good-bye . . ."

"Lady of the Manor stands on the terrace to see the coppers off," Toye remarked. "Quite spoils her set-up, having a murder in the family, doesn't it?"

In the driving mirror Pollard saw Shirley Stanton break her pose with an abrupt movement, and go back into the house.

"Yes," he agreed. "Most untimely from her point of view. Extraordinarily pleased with themselves, that couple. People who look at you with rueful smiles and implied mutual understanding."

"Wallowing in their ruddy alibis, weren't they? The Crown Court, and Colonel thingummy, and the Pensioners' Christmas Tea, and whatever. People of our sort always help the police, don't they?"

"They have got you hipped," Pollard said with amusement. "We'll have their ruddy alibis put under a microscope, but it sounds as though they'll be supported by cohorts of witnesses all along the line. Allchester and Thomas had better investigate the Pensioners' Tea and whatever, and interview the Longstaple couple. The Warhampton chaps can get cracking on Stanton's movements on 14 December. . . . Yes, I absolutely agree that collectively they're an unattractive lot, although I'm sorry for Mrs. Mark. He can't be easy to live with. It'll be interesting to see what the girl Belinda is like. D'you know, Toye, I've got a hunch that she did see Lister in Corbury. If it was late in her vacation, it could tie up with the time he put in at the Allchester archives. If he came over, what for? There's just a chance she might be able to put us on to something: she's high on our list of priorities at Warhampton."

Toye, cautious by temperament, remarked that if the girl thought she'd seen Lister in High Street, it wouldn't be much of a lead.

"Don't be so damn' grudging," Pollard retorted, turning and groping on the back seat. "Where are those copies of today's *Corbury Courier* that Thomas got for us? I want to look through the thing."

The *Corbury Courier* of 8 June had gone to town on the sensational events of recent days. FORMER CORBURY RESIDENT FOUND MURDERED AT ROMAN VILLA, the headline spanning the front page proclaimed with less than perfect accuracy. Below this a sub-heading carried on the story with WELL-KNOWN LOCAL SALESMAN AND HIS SON MAKE HORRIFIC DISCOVERY. A photograph showed the trench where the body had been found, unnecessarily marking the spot with an X. An interview with Horace Rudd was graphically reported, and accompanied by his photograph, in which he looked almost unrecognizably grim. The medical evidence forthcoming at the inquest was quoted in full, with special emphasis on the fact that deceased's skull had been fractured by a heavy blow. Space was devoted to Bernard Lister's early connection with the town, particularly his scholarships gained from the Grammar School. The account of his subsequent career was sketchier, as being clearly of less

interest to Corbury readers. His relationship to the Plowmans was discussed on an inside page in the form of an
interview with Mark.

"We have been out of touch with Bernard for many years,"
he was reported as saying. "After our schooldays our paths in
life took very different courses."

"The bust-up very nicely papered over," Pollard remarked,
who had been reading aloud some of the choicer extracts
from the paper. "Thomas is quite right. This is a good photograph of Plowman: we'll ask Warhampton to produce copies,
and get some off to the Yard for the chaps working on his
alibi. We seem to be making good time. Better stop off for a
bite soon, and aim at turning up at the Warhampton HQ
about two, when people'll be back from lunch."

This programme was followed, and after polite preliminar-
ies and a discussion of the case with Superintendent Norrington,
Pollard and Toye had a lengthy talk with Inspector Worrall.
The latter was unforthcoming at first, which Pollard rightly
attributed to chagrin at having failed to clear up the break-in.
After a time, however, he thawed in response to the relaxed
friendliness of the Yard pair.

"Conclusive evidence, my foot, sir," he said. "To my dying
day I'll swear it was young Tresillian, and probably another
one of that lot from the top flat. They'd know the ground, and
exactly the sort of thing that'd rile a chap like Lister. Putting
his work back, I mean. If there was any loose cash around, I
don't doubt they'd have nicked it but they wouldn't pinch
things they'd have to flog for ready cash. I don't see them
taking that amount of risk of landing up in court again so
soon. Mind you, it wasn't Lister gave us the tip about what
was going on. It was Dr. Halton, the gentleman in the
ground floor flat. But Lister being right underneath, they'd
naturally think it was him."

"Where's Tresillian now?" Pollard asked.

Although the enquiry had been temporarily suspended,
Worrall admitted to having kept unofficial tabs on the students. Tresillian had been sent down for good by the university authorities after his conviction. He had now returned to
Warhampton with the intention of rallying support for his
appeal to be allowed to return in the autumn. His fine had
presumably been paid by his family, and at the moment he
was keeping himself going by odd jobs of casual labour. The
other three residents in the flat, who had received condi-

tional discharges and short suspensions, were back at the university. At the moment Tresillian was sharing digs with one of them, Timothy Parr, whom Worrall considered a likely partner in the break-in.

"He's a bloody insolent type," he said. "Trouble was, you see," he went on, harking back to the difficulty of his enquiry, "when Tresillian's aunt had 'em cleared out, none of 'em had any fixed abode up to Christmas, not really. Trying to pin 'em down for the night of 14 December or any other just wasn't on. They mucked in with friends, one night here and the next somewhere else."

"Fair enough," Pollard agreed. "Suppose Inspector Toye and I have a go? Muscle in brandishing our Yard credentials, merely interested in the break-in because it could throw some light on the date when Lister vanished. Keep harking back to his murder, and trying to rattle them."

Worrall was not optimistic.

"They're as hard-boiled as they come," he said, "absolutely sure they've got us on toast over the job. Still, I won't say that your being from the Yard mightn't give them a bit of a jolt, especially as we've laid off them for some time now."

Later, Pollard and Toye left to inspect Bernard Lister's flat. To avoid getting involved with Mrs. Tresillian, now in residence again after her world cruise, they parked short of the house, and approached it on foot. They saw that a car could drive in, and immediately swing right along some weedy gravel which ran the width of the building.

"Hold on," Pollard said. "These shrubs are quite thick. Would anyone on the pavement see a car if it was parked up against the house?"

"Not after dark, you wouldn't," Toye replied after they had investigated. "Got anything in mind, sir?"

"No, just thinking generally. Lister got to Corbury somehow, either dead or alive. Let's go inside."

They let themselves in at the front door, and went quietly upstairs. After the fresh summer evening Bernard Lister's flat was oppressively stuffy, and Toye opened some windows. In the course of the Warhampton CID's enquiry a semblance of order had been restored in the sitting room. The torn pieces of paper were in plastic bags, the former contents of the desk had been sorted and stacked, and the typewriter retrieved, but the scattered piles of books still lay on the floor. In the bathroom the window was securely boarded up, and the scattered sponges and other toilet articles lay collected in the washbasin, now thick with dust. All food had been cleared from the refrigerator in the kitchen, and its door left open. Pollard looked into the cupboards. At the bottom of one of them was a pile of old newspapers. He recognized *The Times* and, to his surprise, the *Corbury Courier*.

"Looks as though he had it posted to him," Pollard remarked. "Probably so that he could keep tabs on the Millenary plans. Look, something's been cut out of this one."

It was Toye who found the folder of newspaper cuttings as they sat looking through the papers on the desk. About a dozen were clipped together, with an account of Sir Miles LeWarne's funeral on the top. In the list of mourners Mrs. Gerald Stanton's name had been asterisked. A footnote made Pollard and Toye exchange glances.

"Definitely not a well-adjusted personality, the deceased occupant of this flat," Pollard said, examining the rest of the cuttings.

These all related to Sir Miles LeWarne's last illness and death, and included a lengthy obituary, together with tributes from leading Corbury personalities. None gave information about his will, or Shirley Stanton's inheritance. Putting the folder aside, they began to sort another pile of papers. These were mainly reprints of articles which Bernard Lister had published in leading historical journals, and Pollard's attention was diverted to the contents of the plastic bags.

"This is it all right," he said, after examining a series of torn fragments. "The foolscap is rough notes, probably made when Lister was down at Allchester, and the typescript is part of the article based on them which was meant to blow the Corbury Millenary sky-high. Just give me that card of Catchpole's, will you? I'll give him a ring."

Ten minutes later he came into Bernard Lister's bedroom, to find Toye contemplating a drawerful of clean shirts. He reported that his call had made the old boy's day. The Allchester deputy archivist was coming up to see what he could do with the bits, a young chap called Beresford, who'd done some work on early charters.

"Publication will be a matter for Lister's executors, I suppose," Pollard went on, "but from our point of view it might be useful to see exactly what he'd got down on paper. Got any bright ideas from his underwear?"

"Everything a chap uses is still here," Toye replied. "Why

on earth should he have a completely different set of toothbrushes and sponges and whatever for going away? All pretty lush, too. I can't see him going off even for one night with just a comb in his pocket, either. It looks plain enough to me that when he went out of here for the last time, he had every intention of coming back."

"Or else he did come back, and was killed on the premises, the murderer removing the body in a car conveniently parked out of sight down below."

As he spoke, Pollard suddenly felt stifled. The flat and everything in it seemed to close in, enclosing an unhealthily confined space in which resentment and hatred festered.

"Let's get out of here," he said abruptly. "There's nothing more for us to do at the moment."

Over a meal in the grill room of their hotel they debated a late descent on David Tresillian and the friend who had given him houseroom, but agreed in the end to wait until the following morning. As it was Friday night, the odds were that if Tresillian were in work the two of them would be on a blind, blueing his pay packet. Belinda Plowman seemed a better proposition for a visit, but on arrival at her flat they could get no answer. A note addressed 'SUE' was skewered to the jamb of the door by a drawing pin. It read "Away for weekend. Love, B."

"Bet she's gone home," Pollard commented irritably, as Toye pinned up the note again. "Father comes home like a roaring lion after we saw him at the Pottery, and reduces Mother to tears, who rings up her daughter. It looks as though the only thing we can usefully do tonight is to ring the Yard and ask if they've got anywhere with Plowman's alibi."

On returning to the police station he put through the call, and presently came back to the room allotted to them. A limited amount of progress had been made, he told Toye. Plowman had been present at the Ceramics meeting, which had broken up shortly before 3:30 p.m. He had also booked a room at the Hamilton Hotel, Bloomsbury, for the night of 14 December, and the bill for bed and breakfast had been paid on the following morning. Further enquiries were proceeding, but a lapse of six months, and staff changes at the hotel were making things difficult.

Pollard sat slumped at the table, unusually disgruntled, his thick fair hair ruffled and his face flushed in the heat. He had thrown off his coat, and his shirt was creased. Toye, also coatless, looked cool and dapper as always. He studied his superior through his horn-rims.

"Bit early to be feeling up against it?" he suggested.

"I hate this bloody case," Pollard announced vehemently. "It's like a highbrow film on TV, where faces and things materialize out of the blue and float across the screen and off again. You can't see how they really fit in and yet you know you ought to take them into account. . . . Pot-smoking parties, faked charters, a break-in, obscenities scribbled on the account of a funeral—the lot."

Toye waited tactfully to see if there were more to come, and then suggested beer.

"Chilled, if possible and plenty of it," he added.

When he returned with a supply from the canteen Pollard looked up at him with a grin.

"All right, all right," he said, "I'll snap out of it. Half the trouble is the thought of going home to an empty house if we do get back to Town tomorrow. Jane's taken the kids down to my Aunt Is for a week."

Toye seized on this diversion. A year ago they had worked on a difficult case in the area of the redoubtable Miss Isabel Dennis's retirement, and brought it to a triumphant conclusion. They reminisced for a few minutes.

"Here," Pollard said, "we'd better give what's left of our minds to the job on the stocks. The only faint indication of a lead so far is Mark Plowman's unconvincing alibi. I'm sure he could have got here and returned to London the same night. Let's leave motive altogether for the moment and concentrate on opportunity. See if you can borrow an ABC."

They found that a 4:15 p.m. train from Paddington would have reached Warhampton at 6:10 p.m. Return trains ran at hourly intervals up to midnight.

"Opportunity to commit the murder seems O.K.," Toye said. "What would he have done with the body? Left it in the flat?"

"Assuming that he hadn't a car or an accomplice, that seems the only possible answer. Perhaps it isn't as risky as it looks at first sight. If he came down and murdered Lister, they must have been in touch recently, and Plowman could have known Lister was going away the next day. If his alibi falls down, we'll have to find out if he came up to this part of the world again between December and the beginning of the university term."

"Could those students, or whoever broke in, have overlooked a stiff in the place?"

"You wouldn't think so. Quite a useful card to play when we grill them, incidentally. It all rather bears out your theory that Lister went out, all unsuspecting, and somebody saw to it that he didn't go home again, but took a trip to Corbury, quick or dead. Let's go back to Plowman. What conceivable motive could he have had?"

"He made no bones about hating Lister's guts," Toye propounded. "And he stood to lose a fair bit of money over those mugs and things for the Corbury Millenary if Lister published his findings. Some of the souvenirs were going to America, too."

Pollard stretched, and gave a cavernous yawn.

"I can see Lister gloating to Plowman about blowing the Millenary sky high, but all this is absurdly thin as a motive for murder, let's face it. But at this stage one just doesn't know what may come out. . . . We'd better get down to a spot of homework on Tresillian and co. Ask for the case file, will you?"

Later, as they sat looking through it, Pollard suddenly exclaimed and stabbed a name with a biro.

"Belinda Plowman was one of 'em, by God! Now this could link up. The girl smoking pot overhead, Lister in the flat underneath, and Plowman putting two and two together, and making five."

Toye agreed that they had hit on something that looked more like a motive, seeing the aggressive sort of chap Plowman was.

The terrace house where Timothy Parr was living had been converted into student lettings, and had the unco-ordinated and slightly derelict look of its kind. The windows were in need of cleaning, and the curtains a job lot. Two cars were parked in what had originally been a small front garden.

"That's Tresillian's A30," Toye said, indicating a battered model, once pale blue but skimpily resprayed scarlet.

The front door of the house was open, and they walked into a passage hall. A sheet of cardboard fastened to the wall with sellotape gave a list of the tenants and their flatlets, under the heading "HILTON HOTEL," Parr. Flat 3. First Floor, they read, and went up the stairs, to find the name painted in straggling white capitals across the panels of a door. Pollard looked at

Toye, raised an eyebrow, and beat out a brisk tattoo with his knuckles. A languid voice from within urged him to come inside for God's sake.

The room, a pleasant one, running the depth of the house, had been fitted up as a bedsitter, with a small electric cooker and a sink in a cubicle at the far end. A young man was sprawled in a divan bed against the opposite wall, his features largely obscured by a shaggy growth of fair hair. Another, barefoot and wearing only shorts, sat at a table littered with dirty crocks, food, newspapers, a couple of textbooks on economics and sundry miscellaneous objects. Both stared. Before either could speak Pollard took the initiative.

"Mr. Timothy Parr?" he enquired, instinctively addressing the figure at the table. "Good morning. I'm Detective-Superintendent Pollard, and this is Detective-Inspector Toye, both of New Scotland Yard."

He observed the swift chain reaction of defensiveness, unpleasant surprise and in the case of Timothy Parr, assumed facetiousness.

"Wot, no deerstalker?" the latter asked. "No fiddle or foul pipe?"

"Not even a hansom cab at the door," Pollard replied. "The A30's yours, I think, Mr. Tresillian?"

Lying with his right arm behind his head, David Tresillian registered complacency.

"You can't get me on that one. It's licensed, and the insurance is O.K."

Timothy Parr lit a cigarette, drew on it and expelled a mouthful of smoke.

"Worrall sent you along, no doubt," he observed. "A sticker, that bloke. He's been trying to fix the break-in at Imperial Road on us for months. Wants to get his stripes, I suppose. Or don't inspectors get stripes? I wouldn't know."

"Another thing you don't know," Pollard told him, sitting down on a chair brought forward by Toye, "is that the late Bernard Lister was not the person who tipped off the Warhampton police about your pot-smoking in the flat above his."

The silence, though fleeting, was unmistakably startled.

"What bloody right have you got to barge in here and start asking questions and making insinuations?" David Tresillian demanded loudly.

"Don't mind my friend," Timothy Parr cut in quickly.

"He's got a hangover as it happens. Do make yourselves at home, won't you?"

Toye, sitting unobtrusively on Pollard's left, and slightly behind him, remarked that the A30 was a decent little bus for the money. His unexpected entry into the conversation had caused both young men to give him an uneasy glance.

"I expect you found the roomy boot handy?" he suggested.

Pollard watched Timothy Parr's first and second fingers flatten the cigarette held between them. He waited, letting Toye's question hang unanswered in the air.

"Of course, you had better parking facilities at Imperial Road, hadn't you?" he said. "Plenty of room and well off the street. Quite a secluded berth for a car, in fact. Much safer."

"What the hell do you mean, safer?" There was the hint of a rising note in David Tresillian's voice.

"Why, from several points of view, surely. Less obvious to car thieves—vandals. So many of them around these days. And of course very much safer for carrying out a removal that was nobody else's business. Plenty of room to back an A30 right up to the front door, and load directly into the boot."

"Great stuff, this," Timothy Parr remarked to no one in particular, "in fact, rich. Who says the fuzz have imagination? What are we supposed to have lifted from Lister's flat? His bed?"

Pollard let a tense silence build up. Then he leant a little forward.

"Did you look under the bed?" he asked quietly.

There was a sudden convulsive movement by David Tresillian.

"I tell you, Lister wasn't there!" he shouted. "We never set eyes on him."

There was a further pause. Timothy Parr sketched a gesture of humorous resignation, and hummed a few bars of a pop hit.

"I imagine," Pollard said, transposing the interview into another key, "that when you were obliged to leave Mrs. Tresillian's flat, you took the precaution of keeping a key, and also a key to the front door of the house. You may have had these cut, to avoid difficulties with the agent. You knew that it wouldn't be at all easy to find anywhere even tolerably comfortable to live in at that late stage in the university term. I rather think that you continued to spend some time in the flat. It was the middle of winter, and some free heating an advantage. You were quite well acquainted with Mr. Lister's daily programme, and if he came home unexpectedly and cut off your line of retreat, there was always the fire escape, and a bit of wall scaling."

In the absence of any comment, he went on.

"One of these occasions, I think, was on 14 December. No doubt you made sure Mr. Lister was out before you let yourselves into the house. For some reason you decided to take it out of him, wrongly believing that he had been the police tip-off about your drug offences. You went down the fire escape, broke a pane in his bathroom window and got into his flat. There you carried out precisely the sort of damage that you knew would be most infuriating to a man as absorbed in his academic work as he was. Did you"—Pollard's tone changed abruptly from the narrative to the authoritative—"have a look round the whole place before getting down to your vandalism?"

"Yea," Timothy Parr replied laconically.

David Tresillian lay on his back, silently pleating and unpleating the hem of a grubby sheet. Pollard formed an opinion about the nature of his hangover before going on.

"Pot-smoking and bloody-minded vandalism are one thing," he said, addressing himself to Timothy Parr. "Murder is in a different category. Mr. Lister was last seen alive—except by his murderer, of course—during the afternoon of 14 December. You have both tacitly admitted breaking into his flat on that date. At the moment the situation is not particularly healthy for you. If you want to be cleared of suspicion, you would be well advised to be co-operative. At what time did you go into the house?"

"About half-past four."

"What made you sure that Mr. Lister was not in his flat?"

"Oh, for heaven's sake! The curtains weren't drawn, and there was no light in the place."

"All right," Pollard replied. "We'll accept for the moment that you were right, and he was out. What time did he come back?"

The question was shot out with such violence that the prostrate figure on the divan sprang up.

"He didn't come back, I tell you. But a chap who was gunning for him came. We thought he was going to smash the door down."

"What door?"

"The door of Lister's flat," Timothy Parr answered, as David Tresillian had slumped down again and relapsed into silence.

"How did this alleged person get into the house? Surely you locked the door behind you when you went in?"

"No, we didn't. It was never locked during the day."

"Who locked it at night?"

"When we were in the top flat, I think the Halton bloke on the ground floor did. He was always up very late. I suppose Lister did when he was in the house on his own."

Pollard registered this point with interest.

"Reverting to this man who Mr. Tresillian says was gunning for Mr. Lister, he came up to the door of the flat, then?"

"Yea. We were keeping an ear cocked for Lister, and heard somebody coming up the stairs. We'd left the back door open, and legged it into the kitchen, expecting to hear a latchkey being put in the lock. Instead of that, whoever it was started knocking. We were keeping quiet, of course, but some books or something fell down in the study, and the type at the door hammered like mad, and went berserk, yelling to Lister to come out instead of skulking like a rat, and a lot more. We faded out at this point, and went back to the top flat."

Pollard considered.

"Did you have a light on in the study?"

"Nope. Too risky if Lister came back. Anyway, a street lamp shone right into the room."

"What happened next?"

"As we got back into the top flat the racket suddenly stopped, and we heard somebody belt downstairs and out of the house. We dashed over to the window, and just caught sight of a man beating it out into the street. We thought we'd push off ourselves, all things considered, and went down the fire escape, and over a couple of garden walls into the next street."

"Do you know if anyone saw you trespassing?"

"We ran slap into a bloke who yelled after us he was ringing the police. He didn't get much of a look at us, though."

"Could be unlucky for you that he didn't," Toye remarked. "What time was all this?"

Once again, his sudden speech seemed to have an unnerving effect on the pair. David Tresillian turned his head towards the group by the table.

"There was a clock in Lister's study," he muttered. "It struck half past six while we were listening in the kitchen. Made me jump. I hate striking clocks."

Timothy Parr looked uncomfortable.

"Mr. Parr," Pollard said, "you're anything but a fool, and seem to be in full possession of your faculties. From this alleged caller's voice, and what you saw of him, what age would you give him?"

"Wot, me help the police in their enquiries?" the young man replied, having recovered his poise.

"Make no mistake. You're helping to save your own skin, and your friend's over there."

"Can it be that the clever Yard sleuths know who the chap is? Not our age group, anyway. More like yours. Definitely a square. Top coat, and believe it or not, soft hat and briefcase."

"That's all, then, for the present," Pollard said, getting to his feet. "Your statements will be typed out, and brought along for you to read and then sign, if you agree they're a true record of the information you've given."

David Tresillian flung himself on to his face with a convulsive movement.

"I tell you we never saw Lister. You're just trying to pin a murder on us. Oh, God!"

He began to sob.

Disregarding him, Timothy Parr made a detaining gesture in Pollard's direction.

"Hold on a minute. Where do we go from here, now we've admitted to breaking and entering? Isn't it taken into account if you turn Queen's Evidence, or whatever?"

"Under the circumstances, I haven't a clue, Mr. Parr," Pollard replied. "Not my problem, I'm glad to say!"

# Chapter 8

Early on Monday afternoon Adrian Beresford, assistant archivist to the City of Allchester, kerb-crawled along Imperial Road, Warhampton, in his Mini, scrutinizing the numbers on the gateposts. Arriving at number 7, he drove in and parked outside the front door which stood open. He collected his briefcase and walked into the house and upstairs to Bernard Lister's flat, letting himself in with the key entrusted to him at the police station. As Pollard and Toye had done before him, he flung up the study windows.

He stood looking around him, a lightly built young man in his late twenties, with a narrow face, well-cut features and intelligent grey eyes. In spite of its dusty, neglected appearance and the untidy jumble of books on the floor, the room appealed to him. It was the sort of place you could work in. As he picked up one of the plastic bags filled with torn scraps of paper, his attention was caught by the desk, and he bent down to examine it closely. To his astonishment it was the one he had wanted to buy for himself at Baldwin and Young's Saleroom back in the autumn. There was no doubt about it: his exploring fingers found the chip off the right hand corner of the back, which he had vainly hoped might keep the price within his range.

Straightening up again, he addressed himself to the practical problem of working space. He cleared the top of the desk, and after a tour of inspection, returned from the kitchen with a formica-topped table. The job was really a sort of jigsaw puzzle with no picture on the box to help, only one's general knowledge of the contents and wording of medieval borough charters. He extracted some rolls of sellotape and a pair of scissors from his briefcase, and took a lucky dip from the bag containing fragments of typescript. At the sight of words such as *"inspeximus," "Chancery"* and *Corburiensis"* he became instantly absorbed.

Two hours later several oddly-shaped pieces of typescript seamed with sellotape lay around him. One of these consisted of the opening paragraphs of an article on the Corbury charters. There was enough of it to make its tone perfectly apparent. Adrian Beresford was reading it for the third time with raised eyebrows when he was aroused by knocking at the front door of the flat.

He leapt to his feet to answer it, assuming that someone wanted him to move his car. On opening the door he was confronted by a girl in a flowered maxi skirt and white top. She had fair hair, worn long and straight, and blue eyes, but he was immediately struck by her tense expression.

"I'm most awfully sorry if my car's in your way," he said. "I'll come down at once, and shift it."

She made a deterrent gesture with her hand, while continuing to stare at him.

"You can't be," she said breathlessly. "Not the Scotland Yard man. You're much too young. Is he—is he here?"

"Good Lord, no," Adrian replied astonished. "I mean, I'm not Superintendent Pollard. I'm just doing a job for him. I'm Adrian Beresford from the Allchester Record Office. . . . No, he isn't here, I'm afraid. When I picked up the key at the police station they said they were expecting him back from London this evening. Would you like to come in and ring them to see if he's shown up yet?"

As he spoke he realized that the girl was trembling, and on the brink of tears.

"Come on in a minute," he said persuasively.

By the time he had hastily cleared a chair for her, the tears which she could no longer control were running down her cheeks. Adrian took her arm and gently propelled her to the chair, perching himself on one of the arms.

"Why not let up a bit?" he suggested. "There's nobody else here. Then we could try to sort out whatever it is that's bothering you."

She turned her face away from him, and convulsive sobs shook her whole body. Adrian patted her shoulder at intervals, speculating on the nature of the crisis which had reduced her to such a state, and which apparently tied up with a CID Superintendent from Scotland Yard. Presently she steadied herself with an obvious effort, dried her eyes and blew her nose.

"I'm frightfully sorry," she said shakily. "Crashing in on you and behaving like an idiot. I'd better tell you who I am, I suppose. Belinda Plowman. You know. Plowman's Pottery at Corbury."

There was an instant link-up in Adrian's mind. The recent sensational event at Corbury had aroused keen interest in Allchester. But before he could speak the girl was talking again.

"These Scotland Yard men think my father killed Bernard Lister," she said with a kind of flat desperation. "They were cousins and loathed each other, and as it happens, our back gate's quite close to the dig where the body was found. They've been down to Corbury and grilled Daddy. And my aunt, Daddy's sister. And they've found out that I said I'd seen Blister—that's what Daddy and Aunt Shirley called him when they were all kids—down in Corbury last summer. That's why I've simply got to see this Pollard person. He's trying to make out that Blister came to see Daddy, and they had a row. It just isn't true. Daddy was away all that day, down in Cornwall about clay. He—he hasn't seen Blister for more than twenty years."

Adrian detected a different intonation in her final sentence. She's covering up something she's frightened about, he thought. Looking down at Belinda's bent golden head and unhappily fidgeting hands he felt increasingly protective.

"Of course you must see Pollard, and tell him your father wasn't there," he said, applying himself to the immediate problem. "Suppose I ring the police station now, and find out if he's back? I'll go round there with you, if it would help."

To his astonishment she went rigid.

"I can't face it. Not that place. Not after that awful night. . . . You wouldn't know, but I was taken there in a police car. I've—I've been in court, on a pot-smoking charge."

"Mahomet can jolly well come to the mountain then," Adrian replied with decision. "Leave it to me."

Without waiting for any further discussion he put the call through.

"All settled," he told her, replacing the receiver after a brief conversation. "Pollard and his minion are coming along in about half an hour." He straddled a chair, resting his arms on its back, and contemplated her thoughtfully. "You don't look to me like a type who's hooked on pot," he remarked.

"I'm not," Belinda replied indignantly. "I think it's lousy stuff. It was only that once. . . . I was asked to a party. You know . . . one doesn't want people to think one's stuffy or anything," she finished rather lamely.

Adrian felt emotively old and experienced.

"Do you think it's wrong? Pot, I mean," he insisted.

She rubbed her eyes with the back of her hand.

"No, I don't think I do. Not if you don't overdo it, or go on to hard stuff, any more than reasonable drinking's wrong."

"Well, then, why are you so churned up about having smoked the stuff just once? Did the Bench or the police bully you?"

"No. Not the police, anyway. It's not that. Daddy minded so—I'm awfully fond of him. Oh, hell—it's that I'm terrified that because of the court case something ghastly happened, and—and it'll be all my fault if it did."

"Let's have it," Adrian urged. "If something ghastly's got to be coped with, two people on the job are better than one. And I'm safe as houses, by the way."

Belinda slowly raised her head and gave him a long look.

"D'you know, I believe you are. Anyway, I'll blow up if I can't talk to somebody. I'm scared stiff. You see, it's true that Daddy really loathed Blister. He had an absolute thing about him. When the pot case was on, he—Daddy, I mean—came up to hold my hand, although I'd much rather he'd stayed away, of course. Afterwards he took me and the other two girls out to tea at his hotel. I knew that Dave Tresillian, the boy who gave the party in the flat over this one, thought a university don who lived here had brought in the police. But it wasn't until we were having tea that one of the girls said that the don's name was Bernard Lister. . . . Well, I saw the look on Daddy's face, and he knew I'd noticed it, and was jolly careful to say good-bye to us all together. And ever since it came out that Blister had disappeared, he's been different. . . . And, well, he was in London on his own on the night of the 14th of December when the police think Blister was murdered."

Adrian considered.

"So what's worrying you is that on paper your father could have come down here to beat up Blister, and might have overdone it by mistake?"

Belinda nodded, unable to trust herself to speak.

"Did he do this Corbury–London trip by car or train?" Adrian asked, his mind working quickly.

"Train."

"Well, then, how could he possibly have got Lister's body down to the dig at Corbury?"

There was a tense silence. When she answered, her voice was little more than a whisper and he had to strain his ears to catch what she was saying.

"Not then, he couldn't. But—but he drove up to fetch me home for Christmas on 19 December. I'd spent the first weekend of the vac with friends."

"Look here," Adrian said, firmly suppressing his initial shock at the implication of her reply, "are you seriously suggesting that your father drove you from here to Corbury with a corpse in the boot?"

"Put like that it sounds crazy, I know," she said, miserably. "In the middle of the night, though, when you can't sleep, it doesn't seem absolutely not on. Daddy's got a terrific temper. It would have been an accident, of course, and then he might have felt it was better to do absolutely anything to cover it up, because of Mummy and me. He isn't always very—well, sensible."

From below came the sound of a car turning in at the gate and drawing up.

"Pollard, from the look of it," Adrian said over his shoulder from the window. "Now, not to worry. As soon as you're through with him we'll go and have supper, and work out our line. I must nip down and move my bus."

Belinda sat on alone, recognizing with astonishment how very comforting Adrian Beresford's use of the first person plural was. She was so absorbed in this discovery that a tall, fair man, fresh-coloured and with a pleasant, unremarkable face, was walking into the room before she surfaced.

"Miss Belinda Plowman?" he said, coming forward with hand outstretched. "I understand you have some information which may help us. I'm Superintendent Pollard, and this is my colleague, Inspector Toye."

With a feeling of near panic, she murmured something non-committal as he took a chair pushed forward by Adrian, and sat down facing her. Inspector Toye stationed himself near the desk, and Adrian settled himself in the background with a certain deliberation. Belinda sensed that Superintendent Pollard was aware of the manoeuvre and had decided to accept it.

"Well, Miss Plowman," he said, smiling at her, "we're glad to hear anything with a possible bearing on this case, no matter how small it may seem to you."

She braced herself to speak.

"It's about when I saw Bernard Lister in Corbury last September," she told him. "I—I'm quite sure I did see him. I'll swear to it, if you want me to."

"Will you tell us about it as fully as you can?" Pollard invited. "Don't be put off by Inspector Toye's taking notes."

He listened attentively as she described how, when walking up Corbury High Street, she had caught sight of the man whom she had previously studied with such curiosity on a lecture platform in Warhampton. She had stopped and stared at him. He was engrossed by something in the window of Baldwin & Young, the estate agents. Edging nearer, she had stood behind him and looked at the reflection of their two faces in the plate glass. Then, feeling self-conscious and inhibited, she had abruptly turned and continued on her way up the hill without looking back, soon regretting not having made herself known to him.

"A very clear account, Miss Plowman," Pollard said. "Can you remember the date when this happened?"

"Perfectly well," Belinda replied, with a sudden change to aggressiveness. "28 September. My father was away all that day, down in Cornwall about clay. He didn't get back till about seven. And he had one of our people from the Pottery with him: Tom Mawkins, he's called."

She thrust out her chin as she spoke, reminding Pollard of Shirley Stanton. He refused her challenge, passing on smoothly to another issue.

"Thank you," he said. "All things considered, it seems rather surprising that Mr. Bernard Lister was so interested in a Corbury estate agency's window display. Can you suggest any explanation?"

"I haven't a clue."

"May I come in here, sir?"

Three heads turned in the direction of Adrian Beresford on the far side of the room.

"By all means," Pollard invited.

"28 September was the day before Baldwin & Young had a big sale in their auction rooms at Allchester. They'd plugged it in advance all over the neighbourhood, and there would certainly have been a notice of it in the window of their branch office at Corbury. It looks as though Mr. Lister went to the sale, because he bought that desk. I had a yen for it myself, but it soon went through my ceiling. I know it's the same one, because I spotted a chip out of the back when I had a look at it."

"There *was* a poster affair about the sale," Belinda volunteered, Adrian's co-operativeness making her feel slightly ashamed of her recent truculence. "I read it. I was interested because a lot of things from Edgehill Court which had been left to my aunt were in it."

"Thank you both," Pollard said. "This could be a useful bit of information. Just one or two more points, Miss Plowman. I understand that you were away from Corbury on 14 December, the date on which we believe Mr. Lister disappeared?"

"Yes, I was. When term ended on the twelfth, I went home with one of the girls I share a flat with. Her name's Angela Noyes, and she lives in a village called Shipgate, near Norwich."

"Did you spend Christmas there?"

"Oh, no. I went home—to Corbury, I mean—on the nineteenth."

"Rather a cross-country journey," Pollard remarked. "You went by road, I expect. Did you drive yourself?"

He watched her suppress an impulse to look at Adrian Beresford.

"I don't have a car of my own. Mr. Noyes drove me back here and my father picked me up at the flat."

"By car?"

"Yes," she replied a little breathlessly.

"Well I think that covers everything, Miss Plowman," Pollard said after the briefest of pauses, "so we needn't keep you any longer. Thank you for contacting us."

As he spoke, Adrian Beresford got up and came forward.

"Fine," he said, pleasantly but emphatically. "We're going off to have supper somewhere. Perhaps I could just make a brief report on this job as far as it's gone, sir? Here's the car key, Belinda. I'll be down in a jiff."

As Toye closed the door behind her, Pollard picked up one of the reconstituted sheets of typescript, suppressing his amusement at the young man's masterfulness.

"You're making headway with this," he remarked.

"I can state definitely that it's an article on the Corbury charters," Adrian told him, "based on the research Mr. Lister did down at our place. The thing that sticks out is the preamble."

"In what way?"

"It's pure vitriol. He seems to have hated Corbury like hell, and couldn't wait to knock their Millenary celebrations."

Pollard nodded.

"I'll be most interested to see the finished product. When will you be through?"

"Oh, by tomorrow evening, anyway. Do I leave it here for you or drop it in at the police station with the key?"

"We'll let you know about that by mid-morning. Pick up the key at the station again in the morning, will you? Inspector Toye and I are staying on here a bit. Now, we mustn't keep you from your supper date. . . . Have you known Miss Plowman long?"

"I met her quite recently, actually," Adrian replied with brevity. "Good night, sir. Good night, Inspector."

That chap's too bloody quick on the ball, he thought, running down the stairs. The sight of Belinda in his car was surprisingly satisfactory.

"Here goes," he said, swinging himself into the driving seat. "She's not a Jag—third-hand actually—but she gets you there."

As the Mini nosed out into the road, Belinda, suddenly bewildered by the course of events, heard herself announce that she wasn't hungry.

"Well, I hope you won't mind sitting and watching me stoke up," Adrian said. "I'm ravenous. Nothing but a couple of sandwiches and a coffee since breakfast. I thought we might eat at my pub. Only one-star, and you won't get a five-course dinner, but I thought it had the right sort of cooking smells when I clocked in after lunch."

The Black Dog had an unpromising façade on the street, but was unexpectedly roomy and well-found inside. In the dining room Adrian gave to the menu the undivided attention that he habitually devoted to the matter in hand. Finally he ordered ham, eggs, sausages and chips.

"How about you?" he asked, looking across the table. "One's got to eat, you know, come hell or high water."

"Well, perhaps I could," Belinda replied, blushing a little.

"Jolly good. Twice then, please," he told the waitress, and
announced that he was going off to collect a couple of beers.

When the food arrived it was hot and appetizing, and
Belinda tucked in as heartily as her host. The tables were
close together and in demand, and their conversation was
necessarily general, exploring common interests. In occasional
silences she felt guilty at the way in which she was intermit-
tently forgetting her worry about her father. When they had
finished their coffee, Adrian suggested a run in the car.

"The idea isn't what might commonly be supposed," he
added a shade abruptly. "We want somewhere quiet to talk."

"But oughtn't you to be getting on with those papers? . . .
I mean, I seem to be taking an awful lot of your time. . . . I
didn't imagine that was the idea," she concluded incoherently.

"I've broken the back of the job," he said decisively. "Pollard seemed to think it would be O.K. if I finished by
tomorrow night. Come on, let's go. I'm sure you know a
peaceful spot somewhere."

A small pang went through her at the realization that he
might be leaving so soon, followed by a swift realization that
term was practically over, and Allchester was not, after all,
very far from Corbury.

The rush hour traffic had abated, and they were soon clear
of the suburbs. Adrian took a side road, and presently parked
in a gateway. For some moments they sat in silence. Darting
a glance at him, Belinda saw that he was deep in thought.

"I'm trying to think myself into Pollard's skin," he said
suddenly. "We're taking it as read that your father didn't
murder Lister, but naturally Pollard isn't. His job's looking
into means and opportunity and whatever. . . . When did
you come up for your spring term?"

"9 January."

"Did your father drive you up?"

"No. I got a lift."

Belinda forbore to mention that her Warhampton boy
friend of the moment had made a considerable detour to
collect her. Not without gratification she sensed a query in
Adrian Beresford's mind.

"The important point from the Pollard angle," he said,
slowly and deliberately, "could be whether your father might
have driven up to Warhampton again, any time between picking you up on 19 December, and the day the university got
the police to search Lister's flat because he hadn't turned up."

His cool, objective approach both steadied and stimulated her.

"The university started the same day as we did—10 January. I'm absolutely positive Daddy couldn't have come up here again while I was at home: he wasn't away long enough. But"—her voice trembled—"Daddy *was* at home from the fifteenth until he fetched me on the nineteenth."

Adrian extracted a small diary from a pocket.

"We'd better have a look at last year's calendar," he said in a matter-of-fact tone.

As he flicked over pages, he held the diary out in such a way that she was constrained to edge a little nearer.

"Here we are. 14 December was a Thursday. You say your father went back to Corbury on the fifteenth and came up to Warhampton to collect you on the nineteenth. So that would only leave three clear days for another Warhampton trip, and one of them was a Sunday. Don't you think it would have come out in general chat at home if he'd been away again so soon?"

"Yes, I *do*!" Belinda exclaimed, with a degree of relief which he found disquieting "I'm certain Mummy would have said something about it. She fusses so when he's away, even for a day."

Adrian returned the diary to his pocket.

"I don't think you have to worry about this," he said, hoping that Belinda would miss the ambiguity. "We may have a sticky patch ahead, but it won't last for ever."

If this is falling in love, he thought with considerable astonishment, it's a much more comprehensive affair than one ever realized. Not just feeling out of this world, but a sort of joint taking-on of life. . . .

Belinda turned her head slowly, and their eyes met.

"We?" she queried, as if echoing his thoughts.

"Yes, quite definitely we."

"Too much is happening all at once. . . . I just can't take it in."

"Not to worry," Adrian reassured her. "One step at a time. Let's meet for lunch tomorrow, for a start. You'll be at your College place in the morning, won't you?"

"Actually I cut everything today. I couldn't get down to things, somehow."

"There's nothing we can do until we know Pollard's next move, you know. Better to carry on as usual in the mean-

time, don't you think? Let's get hold of some sandwiches, and
go and eat them in a park or somewhere."

He sees things as a whole, she thought, admiration not
untinged with slight alarm. . . . I just get caught up with
whatever's on. . . .

"I'll fix some eats," she said. . . . "We only met each
other about two hours ago, you know."

"What of it? Hours—days—centuries. It's what happens in
a time unit makes it significant," Adrian replied grandiloquent-
ly. His tone changed abruptly. "I say, Belinda, you do like
me a bit, don't you?" he asked, youthful and anxious.

Her murmur of assent was muffled in the sleeve of his
pullover.

"More comfortable like this," he suggested, slipping his
arm round her shoulders, trying to gauge the appropriate
degree of support and pressure.

Silence descended. After an interval he looked down to
find that her eyes were shut, and saw the dark rings of
sleeplessness under them. Some chaps, he thought with
amusement, would be decidedly hipped. . . . A quarter of
an hour later, in spite of a cramped arm, he felt infuriated by
the driver of a tractor which roared and clanked past and
woke her. He announced firmly that he was driving her back
to her flat to get a decent night's sleep.

On the way they decided on a time and place for their
picnic lunch the next day. When they arrived at the flat,
Adrian helped her out, saw her to the door and kissed her
lightly.

"Sleep well, and not to worry," he adjured her, and left.

Feeling dazed, Belinda let herself in. To her intense relief
both her flat mates were out. She was tired beyond the
capacity to think at all clearly, and once in bed fell asleep
almost immediately.

At the Black Dog Adrian sat over a beer in the private bar
until past closing time. He then retired to his bedroom,
where he continued his efforts to reduce his thoughts to some
degree of order.

With a struggle he wrenched them away from Belinda
herself, and tried to focus on Lister's murder. Without a
doubt, Pollard was checking up meticulously on old Plowman. Would he get on to the pot case? If he did, he'd soon
see a possible motive for violent hostility towards Lister on

Plowman's part. And the Corbury police had probably told him already about the family row in the past.

Adrian shifted his position in bed, and stared blankly into the darkness. Suppose Plowman *had* slipped down from London on 14 December, meaning to beat up Lister, and it had ended in Lister being knocked out, and fatally fracturing his skull by landing on a fender or something? There still remained the problem of how he could have got the body down to Corbury. Was it psychologically—or even practically possible, that he collected it when he picked up Belinda on 19 December?

He fell asleep with the question unanswered.

When he woke it was broad daylight. He got up hastily and, having breakfasted and paid his bill, drove round to the police station for the key of Bernard Lister's flat. Here he was handed a message to the effect that Superintendent Pollard would be out of Warhampton all day. Would Mr. Beresford kindly hand in the papers at the police station before leaving for Allchester?

The information made Adrian uneasy. An absence of a whole day suggested a visit to Corbury. Suppose he'd gone down with a warrant for Plowman's arrest in his pocket? Where the hell would one go from there?

It took considerable will-power to concentrate properly on reassembling Bernard Lister's acid article on the Corbury charters.

# Chapter 9

As the front door of the flat shut behind Adrian Beresford, Pollard twitched an eyebrow at Toye.

"Fast worker," he remarked. "What'll you bet that they first met about half an hour ago, when young Belinda came round looking for us, and chanced on him instead? There's a strong whiff of the knight-errant about him at the moment."

"Looks to me like love at first sight," Toye replied solemnly. "It wouldn't come amiss, either. The poor kid could be wanting a knight-whatsit."

Pollard surveyed him with mock concern.

"Romance is getting a grip on you, old son. How come? It must be the insidious effect of the movies, if they have that sort in these explicit days. Gone is your old manly preoccupation with thundering hoofs and the quick draw."

He subsided into a deep armchair. Toye, who relished his ragging, grinned and enquired what he had made of Belinda Plowman.

"I think she saw Lister all right on 28 September. The date really clinches it, after what Catchpole told us. And she's too intelligent to lie about her old man being offstage: it can be checked up so easily. So, what did Lister make that detour for?"

"To see Mrs. Stanton?"

"Let's have another look at these reports that have come in," Pollard said. . . . "Yes, beyond any doubt Mrs. Stanton was in Corbury on 14 December, so couldn't have murdered Lister up here. Of course, she could have been an accessory if her husband did, and then brought the body back in his car. But these Warhampton chaps have checked and double-checked his movements here, and they've been confirmed in every detail. There simply wouldn't have been time for him to meet Lister, work up a row and finally murder him. That couple from Longstaple are unshakeable about Stanton getting home at five past eight. Thomas says the Colonel wanted his dinner, and had his eye on the time."

"Could it have been Stanton that Lister came to Corbury to see on 28 September, then?" Toye suggested. "If they'd been in touch, they might have met by appointment on 14 December. On the road back to Corbury perhaps?"

Pollard crossed his long legs, clasped his hands behind his head and stared at the ceiling.

"It's theoretically possible. On the other hand, this report of Thomas's on the Stantons is pretty comprehensive, as we asked. There's no evidence whatever of their having been in touch with Lister, either over the years or recently. Gerald Stanton is considered a shrewd businessman, but his reputation as a solicitor and as Town Clerk is excellent. His wife is now a wealthy woman and a leader in local good works and whatever. The only adverse criticism seems to be that they're flying a bit high socially since they moved to Edgehill Court. I'm not saying that any of this is conclusive evidence against their being involved in Lister's murder, but a case against them does look improbable alongside this unconvincing alibi that Mark Plowman has put up. Let's look at the notes we brought back from the Yard."

They went once again through the reports compiled by a team of investigators and now somewhat expanded. Mark Plowman had undoubtedly attended the conference of ceramic manufacturers on 14 December, but none of the attendants in the Pottery Section of the Victoria and Albert Museum remembered a visit from him in the late afternoon or recognized his photograph. Taxi drivers from a rank close to the Waterbury Hotel had been humorous at the Yard's expense when asked if they could remember taking a fare to Paddington at about 3:30 p.m. on 14 December. Enquiries at steak houses and news theatres in the Tottenham Court Road area had been equally unproductive. Most unfortunately, the barman at the Hamilton Hotel, who knew him from previous visits, and who could have confirmed the time of his return, had died recently.

"Maddeningly inconclusive," Pollard said. "Let's try working from this end, assuming for the moment that Plowman did come down and kill Lister after the meeting. We now know that he had a perfectly legitimate reason for coming up here on 19 December. This house was empty. Everything we said to Tresillian and Parr about backing a car up to the front door holds good for Plowman. I think it would have been a practical, if risky, possibility to collect Lister's body, if it hadn't been found in the meantime by a cleaner or someone."

There was a silence.

"I suppose a chap with Plowman's background could bring himself to it," Toye said doubtfully. "Driving his daughter from here to Corbury with a stiff in the boot?"

"One's got to remember that he'd got almost foolproof disposal facilities on his doorstep. He could have felt the outrageousness—and the risk—was justified from the point of view of his family."

"What about the girl's baggage?" Toye asked. "Wouldn't she have wanted to shove it into the boot?"

"I doubt it. That age group doesn't go in for organized suitcase luggage. She'd probably just have a duffle bag and an armful of oddments, and chuck them on to the back seat. I wonder."

The telephone rang, shattering the deep quiet of the room. As Toye answered it, Pollard lumbered to his feet and took the receiver held out to him. There was a brief conversation, in the course of which a new urgency came into his voice. The call ended, he swung round.

"They've traced a taxi driver who says he brought a fare to this house from the station at about a quarter past six on 14 December. He remembers it because of one of those perfectly staggering coincidences: his previous fare had been to the house next door."

Toye whistled.

"Have they tried the photographs on him?"

"Yea. He's picked out two, one of which is Plowman's. We'll have to have an identity parade. And what we want now, of course, is evidence of Plowman's return journey to London. The time's crucial."

"He'd have walked to the station," Toye said. "You don't get cruising taxis here, like London."

"This is it. The evening trains from here to London leave on the hour. If Plowman caught the seven o'clock, he's cleared on the students' evidence. Assuming that this taxi driver identified him, he must have been the man they saw going out of the gate just after that clock on the mantelpiece struck half past six. Get it going again, will you, and we'll see if it keeps good time? If it was right—or more or less right—

Plowman couldn't possibly have come back, presumably with Lister, murdered him and got to the station in time to catch that train. But if there's conclusive evidence that he left on a later one, it's a different story."

Toye agreed. They were discussing the chances of getting any such evidence after a lapse of six months when sounds of an arrival below took them to the window. A taxi had driven in, and the two passengers, a dishevelled man and woman, were helping the driver unload a large quantity of miscellaneous luggage.

"Good Lord, it must be the people from the ground floor flat Worrall told us about," Pollard exclaimed. "The ornithologist chap who's been in South Africa since early December. It's worth having a word with him. He might possibly know something about Lister's plans for the Christmas vac, although I rather doubt it."

They shut Bernard Lister's flat once more, and went downstairs to be greeted by chaos in the entrance hall. It was littered with boxes and bundles, among which a giant of a man with red hair and beard was rootling energetically. He straightened up and stared at them.

"Good evening," Pollard said. "You're Dr. Halton, I think? We're Detective-Superintendent Pollard and Detective-Inspector Toye of New Scotland Yard."

"What goes on?" Dr. Halton demanded. "You came out of Lister's flat, didn't you?"

"We did. I gather that you're only just back in this country and have been off the map recently? I'm sorry to tell you that Mr. Bernard Lister has been murdered. His body was only discovered last week, but he disappeared on 14 December."

Dr. Halton appeared to be struck speechless, but only briefly.

"Peg," he bellowed.

A small dark woman, face weathered to the colour of old leather and lank hair strained back in a pony tail, materialized in the doorway.

"Lister's been bumped off," her husband told her. "This is Scotland Yard," he added, indicating Pollard and Toye. "My wife."

"Lister?" Mrs. Halton exclaimed incredulously. "What on earth happened?"

"So far we've no evidence of when and where he was murdered," Pollard informed them. "He was last seen in

public on the afternoon of 14 December. When he didn't
turn up at the beginning of the university term, the authorities asked the police to investigate his flat. They found that it
had been broken into from the rear, but there were no signs
of a struggle. Enquiries were made on a national scale, but
with no result. Finally, Lister's body was found by chance in
an archaeological dig at a place called Corbury, in the West
country. His skull had been smashed in with the usual blunt
instrument, and pathological evidence put his death about six
months ago. I'm glad to have this opportunity of asking you if
you knew anything about his Christmas plans."

They both shook their heads emphatically.

"A clam," Dr. Halton said, "was chatty compared with
Lister. Our contacts were normally minimal. But I'll hazard a
guess about who might have been involved. Not long before
we went off to South Africa I butted in to rescue him from a
chap who was knocking hell out of him, up there on the
landing outside his front door. Remember me telling you,
Peg? You were out, and missed the fun."

"Would you recognize this chap if you saw him again?"
Pollard asked, suppressing his excitement.

"Sure thing. I peeled him off Lister, and held him by the
collar before booting him downstairs. What's more, I can put
you on his track. The top floor here had been lent to some
students who were run in for pot smoking, and the dust-up
I'm talking about was in the evening of the day they'd been in
court. The chap's daughter was one of them, and he'd come
round to beat up Lister, thinking he'd grassed on them.
Actually I had, as I told him."

"I'd like you to have a look at some photographs. This
could be important."

"O.K. Come along in. Light's better inside."

In the living room further chaos was erupting from suit-
cases and boxes. Mrs. Halton helpfully swept a pile of gar-
ments on to the floor, and switched on a table lamp. Pollard set
out a row of half-a-dozen photographs.

"This is the bloke," James Halton said, picking out Mark
Plowman without the slightest hesitation.

The evening's unexpected developments involved setting a
number of enquiries in train involving both the Yard and the
Warhampton CID. Finally, after a belated supper Pollard

and Toye wrote up their notes, and an early start on the following morning was decided upon.

"We'll make for Allchester first and get a warrant for Plowman there. Less chance of a leak that way," Pollard said.

"Do you reckon to pull him in tomorrow?" Toye asked.

"Only if he gives himself away when asked to explain his false statements and two visits to Lister's flat. There are two whacking great holes in the case as it stands. So far we can't prove that he caught that seven o'clock train, nor how he could have got the body down to Corbury."

Before going to bed Pollard made an attempt to get the case off his back by ringing Jane, now home again with the twins from their seaside holiday. It had gone like a bomb to the end, he learnt, and all three had a super suntan. Neither twin had done anything really outrageous, and Aunt Is had been duly complimentary on their upbringing. . . . Would one of those plastic pools be an anticlimax after the Atlantic, did he think?

Later, however, the case and its problems tiresomely reasserted themselves, and he could not get to sleep. Tomorrow's interview with Plowman could easily result in the chap's bringing off a successful bunk, or even committing suicide. . . . Even if he did neither of these things, what real chance was there of really clinching evidence against him turning up? How utterly frustrating and humiliating it would be if the A.C. started trotting out his usual gag about the law of diminishing returns when a case dragged on. One would have to play for time, only it was so damn' difficult to get past the old boy. Not even a moderately convincing alternative suspect.

Pollard's thoughts rested briefly on the Stantons, then began to move from one member of the Plowman family to another, in the manner of a spotlight. It struck him that they tended to run true to type. That Victorian casting out of Lister's mother, for instance, suggested that her parents were climbing the social ladder with the same determination as their granddaughter Shirley Stanton at the present time. Did the male Plowmans tend to marry inept women? Surely Mark and Shirley's mother should have been able to cope with her own children's bloody-mindedness towards Bernard Lister at the nursery stage, and Mrs. Mark was a poor creature by the side of her husband and daughter. Wouldn't modern psychologists say that Mark's fanatical dislike of Lister was really self-hatred, arising from an unacknowledged awareness of his own inferior ability?

These academic speculations were soothing, and before long he fell asleep.

By half past ten on the following morning, Pollard and Toye were at Corbury police station, closeted with an unhappy Superintendent Thomas.

As the complex interrelations of the students' appearance in court, Mark Plowman's assault on Bernard Lister, and his attempt to get into the latter's flat on 14 December were unfolded, the Superintendent's initial incredulity gave way to mounting anxiety. When Pollard came to an end there was a prolonged silence.

"Well, what's your reaction?" he asked at last.

Superintendent Thomas gripped the arms of the chair, and hoisted up his stalwart form.

"Nobody but a fool would deny there's the makings of a case there," he said, and relapsed into silence once more.

"It's over the body being got down here we specially want your help," Pollard told him. "We think it's a practical possibility from the Warhampton end, provided Plowman had the keys of the house and flat. If he killed Lister on 14 December, he could have taken his keys then. We know that he went up to Warhampton on 19 December to fetch his daughter. In your opinion is it conceivable that he brought the body back in the boot?"

Superintendent Thomas shot a glance at him from under the thickets of his bushy eyebrows.

"Knowing the Corbury set-up better than you, if you'll excuse me," he said, "I reckon he could've brought himself to it, feeling it'd be better to risk it for his family's sake rather than chance the job being traced to him by just leaving the body in the flat. One's got to remember he'd got a ready-made grave for it that nobody would notice, and which would be sealed over for good and all. The Plowmans would have been finished here, a leading family for two hundred years back and more. There'd be no living it down, not in a place like this."

He made a gesture incorporating the borough of Corbury. Pollard had a passing claustrophobic sensation of being hemmed in by curious eyes and whispering tongues.

"I get you," he said. "At the same time, we'd like you to

find out if he went off for the best part of the day between 15 December and 9 January, other than on 19 December."

Superintendent Thomas scribbled a note on a pad.

"This is a bloody awful business," he said. "I hope to God you're after the wrong man. Mind you, if he did kill Lister it would've been accidental. Manslaughter, I mean, in a punch-up. Not that a manslaughter verdict wouldn't finish him here in Corbury just the same."

"There's still a vital gap in the evidence against him over the time of his return to London," Pollard pointed out. "If he can prove he caught that early train, he's clear."

"And how the hell can he after all this time?" Superintendent Thomas demanded savagely.

"Equally difficult for the prosecution to prove that he didn't, you know. Well, I suppose we'd better push along to the Pottery, and see what he's got to say for himself. We've got our procedure lined up for the alternative outcome, haven't we?"

Assenting gloomily, Superintendent Thomas showed them to their car. Five minutes later they drew up in the car park of Plowman's Pottery, Pollard remarking that he felt like a cat on hot bricks.

"Pick where you like, and go wrong every time," Pollard said as they walked towards the entrance. "One, we arrest the wrong man. Two, the only serious suspect flees the country. Three, the said suspect commits suicide."

"I'd go for the last," Toye said seriously. "Proves we got the right chap, saves no end of bother and better for the relatives in the end."

The receptionist greeted them with interest, but nothing more, and returned in a short space of time to say that Mr. Plowman would be free in five minutes. There were seats in the reception area, but Pollard wandered around restlessly, inspecting samples of the firm's output, his ears straining for the sound of a car being driven off at speed. How effective were the shadowing techniques of the Allchester CID, he wondered? Then, as he stared at a vast ornate vase in lime green and mustard yellow glaze, Plowman Pottery's contribution to the Great Exhibition of 1851, a bell rang sharply and he relaxed.

"Step this way, please," the receptionist invited brightly.

As they came in, Mark Plowman sketched the gesture of rising.

"Morning," he said briefly, indicating two chairs. "Well, what is it this time?"

Pollard settled himself in a leisurely manner, crossing his legs and looking steadily at the combination of mediocre ability, doggedness and choler in the face confronting him.

"This time, Mr. Plowman," he said, "it's to give you the opportunity of amending various false statements you have made in connection with the late Mr. Bernard Lister. If you wish, you are entitled to send for your solicitor."

A dull flush mounted slowly to Mark Plowman's temples.

"I don't need a damn solicitor, thank you," he said. "I've done nothing criminal."

The wording was unexpected. Pollard turned impassively to Toye.

"Record that Mr. Plowman declined to send for his solicitor. We'll take first your statement that the last time you saw Bernard Lister was twenty-two years ago, Mr. Plowman. We have an eye-witness of a meeting between you at number 7 Imperial Road, Warhampton, in November last, in the course of which you physically assaulted him. Do you deny this?"

Mark Plowman picked up a pamphlet from his desk, stared at it, and threw it down again.

"No," he said. "Obviously you've got on to that hulking red-headed bastard Halton, who butted in on what was no business of his. Incidentally he assaulted me."

"It seems," Pollard went on, deliberately provocative, "that you mistakenly thought Bernard Lister was responsible for your daughter's appearance in court."

"Mistakenly my foot! That's all you know about my late unlamented cousin. It's exactly the sort of thing the little rat would have enjoyed doing out of sheer bloody-mindedness, once he'd discovered Belinda was mixed up in the business. Any decent father would have reacted as I did."

"If you think your conduct was justified, why didn't you admit to it when I questioned you before?"

"For heaven's sake!" Mark Plowman exploded irritably. "Doesn't it stick out a mile? Would you let on that you'd had a scrap with a chap whose body had just turned up a few yards from your back door? And admit that you'd had the worst of it, what's more, because of that swine Halton sticking his nose in?"

Pollard was momentarily silenced from astonishment. Was it possible that Plowman could be guilty if he really equated the finding of Lister's body in the dig with his own discomfiture at being thrown out by Dr. Halton?

"We'll go on to your statement about your movements on the evening of 14 December," he said brusquely. "I put it to you that it was a fabrication from start to finish, and that when the meeting at the Waterbury Hotel ended you went down to Warhampton by train. Do you admit this?"

A more guarded expression came over Mark Plowman's face. "No comment."

"In that case, then, we shall ask you to take part in an identity parade before a Warhampton taxi driver. He took a fare to 7 Imperial Road, at about a quarter past six on that day, and has picked out your photograph and one other from a set of half-a-dozen."

There was a silence. Mark Plowman examined his fingernails. Finally he gave a shrug.

"You win," he said. "All right, then, I did go down to Warhampton after the meeting. There's no reason why I shouldn't admit it. It's alleged to be a free country. I did nothing illegal."

"What was your motive in going?" Pollard asked, an edge on his voice.

Mark Plowman stared at him contemptuously.

"You can't be human. I suppose the police aren't, come to think of it. Bloody holier-than-thous—except the corrupt ones, of course. . . . I wasn't going to let Lister get away with what he'd done to my girl. This time I knew I'd have a clear run: I'd seen in the papers that Halton had gone off on some expedition. Pity the natives didn't put paid to him."

"You've got some curious ideas of what is legal, Mr. Plowman," Pollard remarked. "Beating people up, for instance, and making false statements to the police. And I don't think you realize the seriousness of your position," he added, ignoring an expletive.

"What the hell do you mean?"

"You've admitted going to 7 Imperial Road on the evening of 14 December. Lister was last seen, other than by his murderer, on the afternoon of that day. Six months later his body was found not far from your back door, as you remarked just now."

"So what?" Mark Plowman leant back in his chair, eyeing Pollard with a certain complacency. "Even if I had killed Lister, how do you suggest I got the body down here? On a magic carpet? If you're interested in the facts, I never set eyes on the cad. He hadn't the guts to come out of his funkhole and face me."

"We'll leave the question of how the body reached Corbury for the moment," Pollard said authoritatively. "The facts we're interested in right now are the true ones relating to your movements after the end of the meeting. I may add that we have other witnesses besides the taxi driver."

"All right. Here they are, whether you try to discredit them or not. I went in and upstairs and knocked on Lister's door. He must have spotted me from the window, because he didn't answer, although I kept on hammering."

"How do you know he was there?"

"I could hear somebody inside."

"And then?"

"I yelled through the letter box, and told the bloody little creep what I thought about him. Then all of a sudden I heard the ping noise some telephones make when you ring off. I felt sure he'd dialled 999. So I decided to beat it. I was hopping mad, I can tell you, but didn't want to get mixed up with the police, with Lister gloating on the sideline."

Pollard was briefly silent, remembering David Tresillian's statement that the clock in Lister's study had struck half past six shortly before the man hammering at the door gave up and left the house. He had himself noticed its incisive strike when Toye was setting the clock going. . . . He brushed the matter aside. Everything that Mark Plowman had just said could be perfectly true, and he could still be guilty of Lister's murder. What mattered was whether or not he had caught that seven o'clock train.

"Where did you go when you left 7 Imperial Road?" he asked.

"To the station, of course, to get the next train back to London. I'd looked them up and thought I might catch the one at seven."

"Did you?"

"Just. I wasn't sure of the way and took a wrong turning."

Pollard paused deliberately before his next question.

"Do you really expect us to swallow this highly unconvincing story of yours, Mr. Plowman?"

"I thought you said you wanted the true facts? Well, you've got 'em. Not my fault if they don't fit your book."

Pollard tried a lightning diversion.

"When you arrived at the house, did you look up at the windows of Bernard Lister's flat?"

Mark Plowman stared at him in irritable astonishment.

"What the hell—of course I did!"

"Was there a light in the study or any other front room?"

"I didn't see one. But Lister was there. I tell you I heard him skulking about, and then there was the telephone bell."

"Did you notice if the curtains were drawn?"

"No. I mean, I could see they weren't—if it matters."

"It matters quite a lot, Mr. Plowman. Would Mr. Lister have been in his flat with no lights and undrawn curtains after six on a mid-December evening? Far more likely that you hung about until he came home, followed him into his flat and assaulted him again, only this time with fatal results. You may not have meant to kill him, and were suddenly faced with an appalling problem. You knew the other tenants were away, and that Lister led a solitary life, and decided to leave his body in the flat till you had decided what to do next."

Mark Plowman flung himself back in his chair.

"You're mad," he said at last. "I only just had time to get that train."

"What proof can you give us that you did, in fact, get it?" Pollard asked coolly.

For the first time Mark Plowman looked cornered, and characteristically began to bulldoze his way out.

"How the bloody hell can anyone be expected to prove he travelled on a particular train six months ago?" he shouted. "Try proving I didn't, and see how you get on. Of course it's well known police bribe witnesses to get convictions. I suppose you'll try that."

Pollard remained unruffled.

"If you caught that train as you claim to have done, why not help the course of justice by trying to remember something about your journey? Suppose we begin with your arrival at the station?"

By patient questioning he managed to elicit a few not particularly helpful facts embedded in the angry abuse of a man now becoming seriously worried. As luck would have it, the train had been half-empty, and Mark Plowman had been alone in a second-class smoker. He could not remember if a ticket inspector had come round. No, he hadn't left the compartment, except to go along to the lavatory. There was a buffet car, but he hadn't wanted to eat, and had a supply of cigarettes in his briefcase.

"I was asleep half the time. It had been the hell of a day," he said.

A sort of alibi, Pollard wondered, on the assumption that you didn't drop off to sleep if you'd just committed murder? Too subtle, he decided. *Could* anyone doze off like that after a killing? He soldiered on, and learnt that on arrival at Paddington, Mark Plowman claimed to have gone to the Refreshment Room, and had some beer and sandwiches, before taking the underground to Oxford Circus. Thereafter his statement was identical with his first one.

"Everything that you have told us will be thoroughly investigated," Pollard told him. "And if you can remember anything more about this alleged journey, I strongly advise you to contact us immediately. In the meantime you will notify the police if you wish to leave Corbury, and must surrender your passport."

He expected an outburst, but Mark Plowman groped in a drawer, and tossed the document across the desk where Toye calmly fielded it and checked its authenticity.

"Once more I'd like to know how you suggest I got Lister's body from Warhampton to Corbury?" he enquired, unexpectedly taking refuge in sarcasm. "In my briefcase?"

"On 19 December you made a trip to Corbury and back by car," Pollard stated.

"Do you know what for?"

"I do. To fetch your daughter."

This time the outburst of anger had a quality of outrage which struck Pollard as genuine. It ended with a powerfully expressed wish to wring his bloody neck.

"I merely stated a fact, Mr. Plowman," he replied. "The implication you have been so quick to draw is all yours. Good morning."

Once clear of the building he looked at Toye, and exhaled deeply.

"Courtesy call on the Super, car to Warhampton, train home," he said. "I'm presenting myself before the A.C. sends for me: we've got to play for time. I'm damned if I'm going to let this case go by default. Let's step on it: we may even get that seven o'clock train ourselves."

# Chapter 10

"Intriguing build-up," commented Pollard's Assistant Commissioner. "Out of the usual run. I sometimes wonder if you get your fair share of the bloody, brief and boring cases."

Pollard hastened to reassure him on this point.

"Reverting to this Corbury business, sir," he went on, feeling his way gingerly, "at first all the sub-plots made it look much more involved than it really is. But it was soon obvious that the murderer had to be someone who had links with both Lister and Corbury; and because of the sort of hermit life Lister led outside his work, this seemed to boil down to the Plowmans. I'm prepared to rule out Mrs. Mark Plowman and her daughter absolutely. Mrs. Stanton could only be involved as an accessory to her husband—I don't consider the question of collaboration with her brother arises. As I've explained, Gerald Stanton was in Warhampton on the day of Bernard Lister's disappearance, but on his legitimate professional business at the Crown Court, and his time is accounted for almost to a minute. Even more important, we have not been able to discover any contacts between Lister and himself. This leaves us provisionally with Mark Plowman, with his long-standing violent antipathy to Lister, and his admitted behaviour towards him in November and December of last year. The case against him appears very strong, although I realize it isn't complete yet."

Pollard paused, feeling that he was getting the situation across rather skilfully, but immediately got a quizzical glance from the A.C.

"All nicely in the bag, what?" the latter remarked. "Except, of course, for disproving Plowman's statement about getting clear of Warhampton on that seven o'clock train."

"I think it may take a little time, sir," Pollard replied, as confidently as he dared. "Inspector Longman's got a strong

team on it at this end, though, and the Warhampton CID are
making enquiries at theirs."

The A.C. tilted back his chair and gazed at the ceiling.

"Come off it, Pollard," he said. "You know as well as I do
that the chances of getting cast-iron evidence on Plowman's
return to London that night are about a thousand to one. It
was six months ago. And obviously there's no question of an
arrest without it. Picture the Press and the mass media if we
pulled in Plowman, and his defence rustled up a worthy type
who swore that he was waiting outside the lavatory for him to
come out, and noticed him specially because he looked like
the wife's brother. . . . No, it's not on. And we've got to be
realistic. I'm sorry, as the case has attracted so much publicity, but there's a limit to the time and manpower we can
afford to spend on hunting for needles in haystacks. Take
another week, and if nothing has turned up by the end of it,
the affair'll have to be shelved."

"I take your point, sir," Pollard replied in an expressionless
voice.

"Well, go ahead then."

The A.C. reverted to a vertical position, a signal that the
interview was at an end. He favoured Pollard with a lengthy
stare, a perceptible glint of amusement in his eye.

"You're a damned lucky devil, you know," he added. "It
wouldn't altogether surprise me if you managed to pull something out of this apparent impasse."

Pollard made his escape, irrationally heartened by this
Parthian shot. Before going to lunch he rang Jane.

"The car's having another week's trial, but looks like being
taken off the job at the end of it. It can't make the pace
required."

"Any criticism of the way it's been handled?" she asked.

"None. In fact, I got the impression that the driving had
been well thought of."

"This," she replied bracingly, "is the thing," raising her
voice against the high-pitched babble of the twins. "They're
raring for their meal: I'd better go. The mugs are a smash hit,
by the way, featuring on every possible occasion."

"Good. Be seeing you at some unspecified hour."

Within half an hour he was closeted with Toye and Longman.

"We've got a week," he informed them. "Results by the
end of it—or else. Any developments, Longman?"

As he listened Pollard marvelled as always at the exhaustive thoroughness with which a Yard investigation is conducted. He learnt that with the co-operation of British Rail, all staff concerned with passengers on trains leaving Warhampton for London from 7 p.m. onwards on 14 December were being identified for questioning. A similar enquiry was in hand about the staff of the Refreshment Room at Paddington, but subsequent changes here was slowing down progress.

Pollard groaned.

"What about the Underground?"

"Trouble there's staff shortage and DIY," Longman replied. "Ruddy slot machines shoving tickets at you, instead of booking clerks, for one thing."

"There'd be a ticket collector at Oxford Circus," Toye said.

As the other two talked, Pollard's vivid imagination conjured up travel on the Underground.

"Hold on," he said suddenly. "How much do booking clerks and ticket inspectors take in passengers? Don't they focus on the cash and the tickets? That's what they're concerned with. Not the passenger unless he's tight or something, or can't produce a ticket. Are we concentrating too much on Plowman's actual train travel?"

Longman was disposed to agree, and suggested switching some of his men to the Refreshment Room enquiry.

"Then there's the Hamilton Hotel," he said. "How about having a bash there yourself, sir?"

Pollard hesitated, aware of an In tray piled with paperwork relating to other cases. Longman had already been over the ground himself. The urge to lend a hand himself finally became overwhelming.

"I don't see myself picking up much in your wake, Longman," he said. "Still, we might go along, Toye. Sometimes the same question asked by somebody else does the trick."

Toye remarked that Plowman had stayed at the place before, which ought to help.

"True. Let's have a look at the file."

They mulled over Longman's report. He had found the hotel on the small side and a bit old-fashioned, and deduced that its lease might be running out. Its charges were modest by current standards. The manager had been co-operative, and Longman had interviewed all members of staff who could have been in contact with Mark Plowman. None of

them had any information to offer about the time he had
come in on the night of 14 December.

"I suppose," Pollard said, "we could get a list of all the
guests staying there that night and have a bash at them . . .
Anyway, let's go along. Be seeing you, Longman."

Once again, the manager of the Hamilton was co-operative,
and Pollard and Toye were handed over to the head receptionist, a competent woman called Fenwick, in her fifties.
She undertook to have a list of the hotel guests of 14 December typed out while members of the staff were being interviewed. It was ready for them when they returned to the
reception desk about an hour later, having learnt nothing
fresh.

Miss Fenwick presented the list with an air of finality.

"Thank you," Pollard said, without accepting it from her.
"I'm sorry to take up more of your time, but now I'd like to
run through these names with you. Nobody gets to know
hotel guests like the receptionist. Can you think of any of
these people likely to have been around, say from 10 p.m.
onwards?"

She registered the implied compliment, but was dubious.

"I might make a guess about some of our regulars. . . .
Families with children just broken up for Christmas, who'd
have been to a show, perhaps. What is it, Sue?" she asked,
with an abrupt change of tone.

A girl had materialized at her elbow, thin to the point of
emaciation and engulfed in a massive black sweater. A perky
little face emerged from its polo collar, with sharp grey eyes
accentuated by blue shadow, liberally applied.

"It's that Mr. Plowman this gentleman's asking about," she
began.

Pollard cut in, anticipating a repressive comeback from
Miss Fenwick.

"Remembered something about him, Sue?" he asked
encouragingly.

"She can't possibly," snapped Miss Fenwick. "She only
joined the staff in March."

"He'd lost some papers," the girl persisted. "I saw it in the
Lost Property Book this morning, when I wrote up Mrs.
Potter's pearl earring."

"What an excellent system you have, and how smart of Sue
to notice the name," Pollard commented tactfully. "Perhaps
we might have a look at the entry?"

In a flash a notebook was whisked from behind the black sweater and slapped down in front of him, open at the correct page.

"15.12.72," Pollard read. "Mr. M. Plowman, 4 Edge Crescent, Corbury. Foolscap envelope containing papers, addressed to self."

"What help you think this is going to be to Superintendent Pollard is more than I know," Miss Fenwick told her underling tartly. "Hurry up now, and get those letters finished."

Receiving a smile from Pollard which was to feature in her daydreams for weeks to come, Sue departed, swaying at the hips.

"Was this envelope found, and returned to Mr. Plowman?" Pollard asked.

"Oh, no. That's quite certain. It would have been signed off, with the date of despatch."

Ten minutes later, Pollard was satisfied that short of contacting every one of the fifty odd guests on the list, he could get no help from this source. He thanked Miss Fenwick, and after arranging for Toye to return later and interview the night porter, they left the hotel.

Out of range of the entrance, they halted on the pavement.

"I bet you're on the same tack as I am," Pollard said.

"That envelope?" Toye hazarded.

"Yea. Plowman said he had a briefcase with him in the train, didn't he? As he'd come direct from the meeting, he'd have had his agenda and whatever in it. And he implied that he'd opened the case to get out cigarettes."

Toye nodded, agreed cautiously that since the envelope hadn't turned up in the hotel, it could have fallen out of the briefcase in the train, and been overlooked by Plowman.

"Well then," Pollard pursued, "isn't there a possibility that it fetched up as lost property at Paddington?"

"They don't keep stuff beyond a month or two, as far as I know."

"For heaven's sake!" Pollard retorted. "It isn't the ruddy envelope we want, but the record of what train it came off. If it did."

"The lost property place'll be shut by now. I could go along first thing in the morning," Toye suggested.

"I know it's about ten thousand to one against," Pollard admitted, "but there's just a chance that a porter or cleaner or somebody handed it in, thinking there might be a reward.

Better to go along than ring in: one's less likely to be choked off by some dimwit. I'll be down at the Yard, trying to clear some of my backlog. I'm dropping in now to size things up."

The backlog of work on his other cases turned out to be extensive and comparatively urgent, and brought Pollard back to his desk at an early hour on the following morning. Numerous people wanted to see him, and he had little leisure in which to wonder if Toye could possibly be having any luck. When at last the familiar, serious face with its owl-like hornrims came round the door, he realized without need of speech that the lead had petered out.

"Well, we didn't expect our number to come up, did we?" he said.

Unexpectedly Toye came towards him without speaking. Pollard stared at him.

"What's up?"

"The envelope was passed in all right," Toye told him reluctantly. "Off the 7.0 p.m. train from Warhampton."

"Didn't I tell you that you were a damned lucky devil, Pollard?" the Assistant Commissioner commented. "And so you are, by God. Now then. Lister was murdered. Cut along, and either unearth a motive for that Stanton chap, or bust his alibi, or find somebody you've completely overlooked up to now. And step on it. The blasted papers are picking up the case again. . . . I'm not actually setting a time limit on the enquiry now, as things have turned out."

"Thank you, sir," Pollard replied. "I think the most practical move is to return to Warhampton as soon as possible."

By the time he reached his own room he had mentally farmed out the bulk of his backlog, and within a couple of hours was on the road once more with Toye. After lengthy discussion they agreed that the least unpromising line of action was a thorough search of Bernard Lister's flat and its contents.

"No aspersion on Worrall and his boys," Pollard said, "but they're human like the rest of us, and could have missed something. After all, Lister was an academic, given to putting pen to paper. If anything was afoot between him and Stanton— or X—I can't help feeling that there's a note or a diary entry, even if it's a cryptic reference."

On arrival at Warhampton there was an inevitable holdup while Superintendent Norrington was brought up to date on the case. This accomplished, Pollard and Toye looked in at their temporary office. Bernard Lister's article on the Corbury charters, skilfully pieced together by Adrian Beresford, was lying on the table.

"I'd better skim through this," Pollard said. "It won't take long. Anything linking Lister and Corbury could be significant."

Within moments he was absorbed, temporarily oblivious of the case. Toye, when treated to a summary, was more scandalized by the turpitude of the fifteenth century Corbury burgesses than impressed by Bernard Lister's scholarship.

"Slack lot they must have been up in London, too," he said disapprovingly, "not to mention taking bribes."

Pollard was amused.

"Well, one thing, Lister's worst enemy couldn't accuse him of slackness. You realize that all this hinges on a copyist's error over one letter, turning Spinner into Skinner? I'll just try to catch Beresford at the Record Office, and tell him he's done a good job."

Adrian Beresford was clearly much gratified by the call. Behind his modest disclaimers, however, Pollard sensed an anxiety which only just stopped short of a direct question.

"I—er—I seemed to have a sort of tie-up with the whole business," the young man proffered tentatively. "Lister working here on the documents, and buying that desk I wanted. I don't know if it's of any interest but he bought some of Sir Miles LeWarne's books, too. I found one or two with the old chap's bookplate when I took a quick look at the heaps on the floor. The Librarian here bought in some. . . ."

Pollard pleasantly but firmly declined the gambits and rang off.

"I'd like to put that pair's minds at rest, not to mention that blundering hothead, Plowman's, but it's too risky. It might leak out, and alert Stanton or A. N. Other. Got the key? Let's go, then."

Bernard Lister's flat felt increasingly dirty and dreary. As they stood in the disordered study, Toye remarked that it was hard to know where to start.

"In here, anyway. One can feel that this was the hub of the poor chap's universe. Let's clear the decks a bit first. Get the books back on the shelves for a beginning. It doesn't matter what order they're in."

"Blimey," Toye said, immediately heaving up a Liddell and Scott Greek Lexicon, "this'd take a bit of reading."

"It's a dictionary," Pollard told him absently, his attention on a mint volume of Gibbon's *Decline and Fall of the Roman Empire* containing Sir Miles LeWarne's bookplate. He surfaced reluctantly and began to tackle his share of the work.

It was by chance that his eye lighted on a book covered in brown paper. The next moment he experienced a sharp tingling at the base of his spine. Neatly inscribed in block capitals was a title: THE LETTER KILLETH. R. LE SPINNER.

He opened the book, and saw the LeWarne bookplate. Turning to the title page he found that he was holding a copy of Anthony Trollope's *Framley Parsonage*. On ruffling through the pages he came on two folded sheets of paper.

"Let's have the forceps," he said abruptly.

Toye produced them from Pollard's working case in seconds. The papers were extracted and carefully opened out on a piece of blotting paper. Chairs were pulled up to the desk.

One document was a sheet of expensive writing paper engraved with the Edgehill Court address. It was headed in an elderly hand 'Gerald Stanton. Final notes for my new Will. 5.12.1971.' Pollard read them to the end, and became aware that he was holding his breath. Beside him Toye was apostrophizing his Maker.

"Easy," he said. "This could be a pointer, but it isn't evidence within the meaning of the Act."

The second folded paper was of different quality, and looked as though it had been torn from a pad used for rough notes. It was a list in Bernard Lister's handwriting of dates relating to the last weeks of Sir Miles LeWarne's life, some of them prefaced by question marks.

"We have been here before," Pollard muttered. "Those cuttings from the *Corbury Courier*. . . ."

Toye unearthed them from a pile of papers on a chair. Within a few minutes it was clear that the list had been compiled from them, and was accurate.

"Rum to think of Lister's happening on this one book by pure chance," he commented.

"Almost incredible," Pollard agreed. "I've wondered if things like this really are chance, or if there are subtle connecting links we just can't see. Anyway, Lister obviously found the papers, perhaps when he unpacked the books and looked them over. From then on it's easy to see how his mind worked. He saw from the cuttings that the young LeWarnes

were killed on 20 November. The final notes for the will are
dated 5 December, so Sir Miles had had plenty of time to
think things over, and come to a decision about the house
and his residuary estate. Then on 12 December he has a
stroke. On the thirteenth he signs a will with a different
principal bequest, and promptly dies from a second stroke.
Highly convenient development for the Stantons."

"Do you think Lister confronted Stanton, and threatened
to contest the will on grounds of undue influence?" Toye
asked.

Pollard was silent, startled by an idea which had suddenly
presented itself to him.

"It could be," he said at last. "Unless, of course, he'd gone
a step further, and suspected that Stanton had submitted a
forged will for the genuine one, and that LeWarne hadn't
been in a state to question what he was signing."

Toye emitted an astonished whistle, his expression one of
combined admiration and alarm.

"All right, all right," Pollard grinned, and pulled the telephone towards him. "We'll play it cool: not to worry. I admit
it's a bit steep. But I'm going to ring the Yard, and ask them
to phone through the full text of LeWarne's will as early as
they can tomorrow. We'll at least know for sure then if
Stanton drew the thing up."

This done, they systematically worked through the rest of
the books, and closely examined the desk for possible secret
compartments, but without discovering anything of interest.
Eventually they sat down again, and lit cigarettes.

"If Stanton murdered Lister to shut his mouth," Pollard
said abruptly, "it was a carefully worked out affair. They must
have been in contact before 14 December. How, when and
where? If we could get on to that, we'd be halfway home. If
you'd been Lister, with blackmail, or just anti-Plowmanship
in mind, how would you have made contact?"

Toye considered carefully.

"I'd have phoned in for an appointment at his office, saying
I was a client, and put on dark glasses and pads in my cheeks
or whatever, in case some Corbury old-timer spotted me."

"If Lister tried that, Stanton's secretary must have made a
note of the appointment, and seen him. However, that's
several stages ahead. Let's concentrate on 14 December. If
Stanton killed Lister, I think we can take it that it happened
then, when he—Stanton—was up here for his client's Crown

Court case. Up to now, his tight time schedule has been his alibi. But if it was a prearranged meeting, following on an earlier one, for Stanton to hand over a signed confession of fraud, or lolly perhaps, well, obviously the time factor's much less important."

Toye suggested a meeting somewhere on the road back to Corbury.

"Don't forget that Lister had turned in his car for servicing before Stanton's case was over. Of course he might have gone to an agreed place by public transport. Less conspicuous in some ways than parking one's car. . . . I suppose they didn't meet at Stanton's car in the Grand Central Hotel car park? It sounds an improbable place for a murder. Would Lister have been fool enough to get into Stanton's car?"

"You'd hardly credit it," Toye said thoughtfully. "But then, Lister doesn't strike you as a chap having his feet on the ground, for all his brains. Living in a sort of fantasy world about Corbury and the Plowmans, anyway."

"You've got something there. . . . Well, the obvious step is to go and look at the car park. It's too late tonight, and anyway, we ought to see it in daylight to get the hang of the place. What's in your mind?"

"Talking about parking's reminded me of the Stantons' old house, sir. We looked inside their garage, if you call it to mind. Nice weatherproof building, but it wouldn't take more than a couple of cars. Didn't Mrs. Stanton say they heard her husband draw up just when they'd started their dinner? Well, did he leave his car outside all night? If the visitors' car was in the garage with hers, seems he must've."

"I think this is important," Pollard said, hoisting himself into a more upright position, and recrossing his legs. "If it was the visitors' car that stood out overnight, Stanton would have had a perfectly sound reason for going out again, and driving his own car round to the garage. It wouldn't have taken him long to heave the body out of the boot, and dump it in a corner under a tarpaulin or something, ready to be shifted to the dig at the first suitable moment. After dark the next day perhaps. . . . I think a visit to those people is called for. Hayter, they were called, weren't they, and lived at Longstaple?"

Toye consulted the file.

"Yes," he said. "Name of Hayter. Colonel and Mrs."

Pollard relapsed into a lengthy silence, frowning as he sat with legs outstretched, drawing on his cigarette.

"If Stanton killed Lister, we're moving into a highly dangerous situation," he said at last.

"You mean he might do a bunk?" queried Toye.

"I mean the hell of a lot more than that. This time he'd have two crimes to cover up, murder on top of fraud. What price the life of anyone in a position to give damaging information? His secretary, for instance, if he got to hear we were showing interest in his office staff? We can't watch our step too carefully."

# Chapter 11

Just before ten o'clock on the following morning Toye drew up at the threshold of the Grand Central Hotel's forecourt.

"If this is the only parking space they've got, we're wasting our time," Pollard said. "No, look. Round the side of the building. 'To Car Park.'"

Toye advanced cautiously, circumnavigating a mound of luggage in process of being loaded into a Mercedes-Benz. They emerged into an unexpectedly large space with an exit to a side street. He drew up and they sat taking in the lie of the land. Apart from a laundry van unloading at the Grand Central's back door and ten or a dozen cars in a section reserved for staff, the place was almost empty.

"A lamp over the back door and a street lamp quite near the exit," Pollard said. "I can't see anything else in the way of lighting."

"You'd get a certain amount from the windows," Toye pointed out.

"Just on five on a mid-December evening. . . . We ought to have come along here before. It's made for assignations at that hour. Stanton arrived in the morning, and could more or less pick his stance. Near the exit, so that Lister wouldn't have to wander around, but not too near that street lamp. With any luck there wouldn't be another car anywhere near: too early for the bar, and shoppers and so on would have pushed off."

"There could be staff coming and going at any hour," Toye objected.

"You are a Devil's Advocate, aren't you? I didn't say it wasn't risky: murder usually is; only that it was a practical possibility. I can picture it easily. Something said to distract Lister's attention, and the blunt instrument in action. Open the boot: Stanton would have backed in on arrival, of course;

144

and heave in the body. Not too difficult for a chap of Stanton's physique, considering how undersized Lister was. Anyone seeing you would think you were loading a sack of potatoes or something. Then drive off, not forgetting to chuck the blunt instrument over a suitable hedge at some point. Let's see what that side street's like."

It was one-way and flanked by double yellow lines, and led them back to the main road at the front of the hotel.

"Lister ran an account at that garage where he kept his car," Toye remarked, as they waited at traffic lights. "I saw some receipts with his papers."

"Come again," Pollard invited.

"I was wondering if he filled up before going down to Corbury to see Stanton. Might be useful to see if there's anything to suggest he made a longish trip in late November or early December."

"That car fixation of yours has got its points. Let's go along."

They found the garage within a few minutes' walk of Imperial Road. It was a small business and the proprietor, a bald tubby extrovert, was impressed by Pollard's official card and anxious to help.

" 'sright," he said, after hunting through a dog-eared day book. "30 November last. Five gallons and half a pint: Mr. Lister, for first thing tomorrow. Tyres would've been done, too, but we don't make a charge, not with petrol. All right?"

"It could be very useful," Pollard told him. "I suppose you don't happen to remember if Mr. Lister said where he was going?"

"He never," the proprietor said emphatically. "Very close little gent, Mr. Lister. Good payer though. Nearly six months the lawyer's kept me waitin' for this last lot. Now Mr. Lister, he paid monthly, regular as clockwork."

Pollard thanked him, and the Hillman once more headed for the police station. On arrival he was handed a lengthy typewritten message which had just been telephoned through from the Yard.

"LeWarne's will," he told Toye, quickly running his eye down the page. "Drawn up by Stanton and Mundy of Corbury. Executors likewise Stanton and Mundy."

He sank on to a chair, and read the details of the will with a mounting excitement which he tried to hold in check.

"Pointers aren't evidence," he reminded himself as much

as Toye. "Time now to be moving in and taking some calcu-
lated risks, from the look of things. Longstaple and the Hayters
for a start."

Toye looked surprised.

"That question of where the three cars—Stanton's, his
wife's and the Hayters'—were parked on the night of 14
December is worth following up. Did Stanton go out after
dinner, saying he'd got to shift his? If he did, he could have
got Lister's body out of the boot, and stowed it somewhere
for the time being. Garden shed, for instance."

"When do you suppose he dumped it in the trench?"

"God knows. One step at a time. Let's get moving."

It was mid-afternoon when they ran into the pleasant little
town of Longstaple, fifty miles beyond Allchester. A courtesy
call at the police station involved a brief delay, but Pollard
was punctilious in his relationships with a local force. Over a
cup of tea in the Super's room he learnt that the Hayters
were one of the numerous retired couples in the area, absorbed
in the characteristic activities of their age-group and social
class. They were in no way remarkable, and lived in a nice
little place called The Rowans on the outskirts of the town.
Keen gardeners, both of 'em, the Super concluded.

Pollard and Toye found the house without difficulty. The
front door stood open, but they had to ring twice before a
man emerged from a door on the right of the hall, wearing
disreputable trousers and an open-necked shirt. He had a
decisive face, with a projecting chin and bulging brow, and
paused to size up his callers.

"Colonel Hayter?" Pollard asked, producing his official card.
"Could you spare us a few minutes?"

The colonel inspected the card with a faintly mystified
expression and returned it.

"Come along in," he said, and led the way across the hall
to a small untidy den. "Hope you haven't been ringing long.
You can't always hear the bell in the garden," he added,
dislodging an outraged tabby cat from a chair, and removing a
pile of old newspapers from another. "Penny's just dropped.
You're on this rum Corbury case, aren't you?"

"I am," Pollard replied. "It's in connection with it that
we've come along, on the off-chance that you might possibly
be able to help us. We're interested in the movement of cars
anywhere near the Roman villa excavations on the night of 14

December last year. You and your wife were the guests of Mr. and Mrs. Stanton, I gather, and had come by car?"

"Quite correct. We're old family friends, and sometimes break our journey with them if we're driving down from town. I'd been up for a regimental dinner. Smoke?"

"Thanks. Did you go on the next day?"

"Yea. We left about half past ten, as far as I remember."

"Did it cross your mind that somebody might have used your car during the night?"

"Good God, no! Never entered my head. Anyway nobody could have after Gerald Stanton had put his own car away, and locked the garage. I mean the place wasn't broken into."

Having by a stroke of luck got the one essential fact he wanted, Pollard angled skilfully for further information.

"One can't altogether rule out the possibility of some unauthorized person having got hold of a key," he said thoughtfully. "There was absolutely nothing to suggest that your car had been taken out? Petrol a shade lower than you remembered, or mud on the floor?"

"Absolutely nothing," Colonel Hayter echoed emphatically. "And I'm certain my wife would have remarked on it if she'd noticed anything of the sort. I'll ask her to come along, if you like."

Mrs. Hayter, a plump cheerful brunette some years younger than her husband, was duly fetched and expressed complete agreement.

"What a horrid thought!" she exclaimed. "A murderer using our car! I'm so glad it was safely under lock and key all night. We sometimes insist on leaving it out, as the Stantons' garage will only take two, but by good luck Mrs. Stanton's was in dock. Good luck for us, I mean."

"Annoying for her," Pollard agreed. "An almost new Austin Mini Clubman, isn't it? I remember noticing it."

"I think her husband was being fussy about the clutch. She said she hadn't found anything wrong with it. I expect he'd got an eye on the guarantee: the legal mind, you know."

"To be absolutely accurate, our car wasn't under lock and key all night," Colonel Hayter interposed. "We ran it into the garage when we arrived just before six, but left the doors open for Gerald. He was late back, and his car was outside the front door until we all turned in about eleven, when he put it away."

"It's the latter part of the night we're interested in," Pollard said. "Did you by any chance hear any activity going on in the lane at the back of the house? Which way did your room face?"

"Over the garden and the lane, but I was dead to the world and didn't hear a thing all night. You, too, weren't you, Jean?"

"Flat out," she agreed. "We all overslept, actually, and didn't sit down to breakfast until half past nine. Mrs. Stanton, who's the world's most efficient housekeeper, was frightfully apologetic, knowing we wanted to get off in good time."

"Gerald Stanton has damn' good whisky," remarked her husband. "It must have been our nightcaps that knocked us out, on the top of a pretty hectic day all round. Talking of drinks. . . ."

On the pretext of having urgent calls to make, Pollard politely declined.

"We must push on, I'm afraid," he told the Hayters, getting to his feet. "I know, of course, that I needn't ask you both to treat this visit of ours in the strictest confidence. If anyone understands about security, it's the Army."

"You've said it," Colonel Hayter replied, unconsciously drawing himself up.

On the road from Longstaple to Allchester, Pollard and Toye agreed that the spate of information produced by the Hayters was almost suspicious.

"I'll swear they're both a hundred per cent genuine, though, wouldn't you, sir?" Toye asked.

"Yea," Pollard agreed. "It's unimaginable that Stanton roped them in as accomplices. Let's do a recap. Hayter's regimental dinner in London must have been a stroke of pure luck for Stanton, making it possible to bring in a couple of witnesses to the time of his return from Warhampton, and the rest. It looks as though he wangled Mrs. Stanton's car being off the premises, so that his own could be in his garage overnight with the Hayters'. Otherwise it might have had to stand out in the road, out of politeness to the visitors, making it impossible to cope with Lister's body."

"Looks like things are falling in," Toye conceded with cautious satisfaction. "Then those nightcaps doped, so that he could get on with the job."

"This is it. Plenty of sleeping pills around these days, and Stanton as host would have dished out the drinks. Did he doctor two or three of them, I wonder?"

"Do you think Mrs. Stanton's been an accessory all through?"

"Impossible to say at this stage. . . . Reverting to that night, Stanton would have allowed time for the dope to work, and then gone quietly out by way of the garden, and got going. The moon was in the first quarter, so he'd have enough light at that hour without risking a torch. And of course he'd have made preparations beforehand: shifting some of the soil in the trench, for instance."

"Rigor would have been fairly well established by midnight, wouldn't it?"

"Yes. I think he would probably have managed to get the body out of the boot when he put the car away, and lined up something in the way of a well-oiled wheelbarrow from his garden shed."

They relapsed into silence. A couple of miles further on Pollard abruptly shifted his position.

"With all this circumstantial evidence, I'm now morally certain that Stanton murdered Lister," he said. "I'm just as certain that we'll never get direct evidence of the murder. I can't believe that with all the publicity there's been any witnesses from Warhampton or Corbury wouldn't have come forward. And any material traces will have gone long ago, with the Stantons having left the Edge Crescent house and other people living there for several months. I bet Stanton's changed his car, too, after giving the boot the full treatment. Of course, the murder presupposes the forgery, and I'm pretty confident that once the experts are turned loose on the papers they'll nose it out. If the papers aren't forthcoming, well, that'll speak for itself. We've got the evidence that Lister found those notes of old LeWarne's, and instantly became suspicious. What it's absolutely essential for us to do is to prove that there was contact between Lister and Stanton."

Toye agreed, slowing down as they came to a village.

"Looks like tackling the office staff's the only way to do it. If any old stager in Corbury had spotted Lister around, according to the Super it would have been the talk of the place in next to no time."

"This is it. And as I've said before, it's dicey. Quite apart from, say, Stanton's secretary's personal safety, nobody can absolutely guarantee he won't give us the slip and make for a handy numbered account in a Swiss bank and some place where he'd be non-extraditable. . . . Good Lord, look at the Oldest Inhabitant stepping in front of a moving car . . . the

chap's managed to pull up, and now the old boy's shaking his
fist at him."

Toye commented caustically that ninety per cent of British
pedestrians still thought we were in the horse and cart age.

"Thanks to that bright idea of yours about Lister filling up
his car ahead of a long run, we've at least got a possible date
to work on," Pollard resumed, as they emerged into open
country. "But I'm not going any further until I've talked
things over with Engle, or another of our tame legal consul-
tants back at the Yard, and put the whole thing to one of the
Fraud Squad boys. If I get the green light, and any sort of
lead from Stanton's people, I'm going to charge him with the
murder, and hope for the best. We'll get a decent night's
sleep at Allchester, and go up by the first train tomorrow."

At Allchester they put up at the Cathedral Hotel. As they
sat over their coffee in the lounge, Toye discovered a copy of
the week's *Corbury Courier*, and studied its contents with
interest. Presently he showed Pollard a conspicuous item
under FORTHCOMING EVENTS.

### EDGEHILL COURT
### CORBURY
GARDENS OPEN TO THE PUBLIC ON
SUNDAY, 17 JUNE, BY KIND
PERMISSION OF MRS. GERALD STANTON
2:00 P.M.—6:00 P.M.
REFRESHMENTS, PLANT AND PRODUCE STALLS
ADMISSION 10p. CHILDREN 5p.
PROCEEDS TO CORBURY MILLENARY FUND

"From the look of things," Pollard commented, "Mrs. Gerald
has now completely identified herself with the Lady of the
Manor image."

Old Bryce, who had stayed on as gardener at Edgehill Court,
conceded that the roses had never made a better show.

Standing in the rose garden during a tour of inspection on
Sunday morning, Shirley Stanton was in a state of euphoria.
This colour, this form and fragrance suffused in midsummer
sunlight, was hers. Hers to share at will with the people of
Corbury. She looked across at her old home in Edgehill Crescent, part of another life, and then at the spill of houses down
the scarp to the vale below. A glow of warmth towards their

inmates pervaded her: the LeWarne mantle was about her shoulders.

On the upper terrace she walked the length of the magnificent herbaceous border. Its discreet information labels enabled her to converse adequately, if not fluently, with the gardening enthusiasts of her widening social circle. A signposted path through the shrubbery brought her out to the paddock. Here a tea bar and stalls selling plants and produce in aid of the Millenary Fund were attractively laid out. An ice-cream cart to be manned by Belinda Plowman stood under a gay umbrella. At the sight of it Shirley Stanton frowned slightly. Would Belinda have that young man from Allchester in tow? Really, it would be most unfortunate if she got herself talked about with somebody of that sort. . . . Reviewing potential alliances with the County circle, Shirley returned to the house.

Gerald Stanton was checking piles of small change, and looked up as she entered his study.

"I've done the floats," he said.

"Good," she replied. "Everything seems to be all right. We'd better have lunch. It's all cold, I'm afraid."

In the Plowman household lunch was already in progress.

"Some more gooseberry fool, Adrian?" Monica asked.

"I'd love some, Mrs. Plowman. It's super," he told her, passing up his plate.

As she ladled out a generous second helping, Monica reflected that the young man was at least clean and his hair reasonable for these days. All the same he really shouldn't come to lunch with comparative strangers in quite such unconventional clothes. She had already sensed unerringly that this affair of Belinda's was different from any of its predecessors, and gave a little sigh. He wasn't at all the sort of bridegroom she had always pictured for Belinda. . . . If only she could talk to Mark about it, but he had been so worried and remote lately. It couldn't be the Pottery: even Shirley was pleased with sales. So it must be this dreadful business about poor Blister. Surely the police would catch the murderer soon, and then it would all die down. . . .

Surfacing with an effort, she suggested that it would save time if they had coffee at the table.

As Mark Plowman drove his party over to Edgehill Court half an hour later, Belinda's spirits were more buoyant than for some time. After all, she told herself, nothing more had been heard of the Scotland Yard men for nearly a week. Moreover, she was young and in love, and it was high summer. On arrival she found her aunt's guarded welcome to Adrian amusing.

"Aunt Shirley's a decent sort, really," she assured him as they headed for the paddock. "It's only that being left this place has gone to her head a bit. She'll get over it in time."

When he did not answer she looked round a little anxiously.

"I say, you weren't hipped by her, were you?"

"Good Lord, no!" Adrian hesitated a moment. "I say, there's something I think I'd better tell you, just in case anything blows up."

Belinda stopped dead, conscious of a painful constriction somewhere in the region of her heart, and of brightness having fallen from the air.

"Pollard's around," Adrian said. "The Hillman they had at Warhampton overtook me at the bottom of High Street before lunch. It turned into the police station. There were four chaps on board."

"Four?" she heard herself echo pointlessly.

"Oh, there you are, Belinda." Emerging from the shrubbery path, Gerald Stanton held out a small canvas bag. "Afternoon, young man. Nice of you to come along and lend a hand. Here's your float, Belinda: two quid. Why are you both looking so worried?"

Good-looking, tall and cheerful, he smiled down at them. Belinda suddenly craved his reassurance.

"Those wretched Scotland Yard men have turned up again," she told him. "Adrian saw them drive into the police station when he came over to lunch. It—it would be so beastly if they came up here."

There was a silence so brief as to be almost imperceptible.

"I should think we can rule that one out," Gerald Stanton said. "We've already given them all the help we can. The poor devils have to slog on with the investigation, you know. Good Lord, people are arriving already. Time to take up action stations."

At Corbury police station little more than a mile away, Superintendent Thomas's room was uncomfortably congested by the presence, in addition to his own, of Pollard, Toye, Superintendent Hart of the Allchester CID and a Mr. Engle, a legal expert frequently called in by the Yard. In spite of open windows the air was stuffy and smoke laden, and the room crumby from a working lunch of sandwiches and beer. In mid afternoon a constable entered in response to a bark from Superintendent Thomas. He saluted smartly and stood to attention.

"Miss Mavis Fletcher, Mr. Stanton's secretary, is on holiday, sir. She's down at Fairport, helping at St. Christopher's Holiday Home for Disabled Persons, and not expected home till next Saturday. I had it from her aunt, Mrs. Walston of the new Pottery shop, who she lives with."

Pollard briefly raised an eyebrow in Toye's direction.

Superintendent Thomas, still looking stunned from Pollard's recent disclosures, nodded abruptly, and the constable withdrew.

"So what?" Pollard said. "I suppose Inspector Toye and I had better go over and see if she can tell us anything about a phone call or a personal visit to the office by Lister. Care to come along for the run, Engle?"

Superintendent Hart tactfully suggested coming too, adding that Thomas would be glad to see the back of them all for a bit.

From a brisk start the Open Afternoon at Edgehill Court had built up to an outstanding success. A properly appreciative crowd of Corbury townspeople wandered about the garden, sat and contemplated, spent money freely on refreshments and at the stalls, and were chatted up graciously by Shirley Stanton, and more informally by her husband. The ice cream cart was besieged, and Belinda and Adrian were under such pressure that any apprehensions were temporarily submerged. Shortly after five o'clock their supplies ran out, and they thankfully closed down.

"Collect up the cash, and we'll hand it in and go and have a wash," Belinda said.

Adrian complied.

"Change your mind about being engaged?"

"No," she said. "Not till we know Daddy's O.K.—or not. I can't give my mind to it. Don't be hipped with me."

"I'm not," he said.

They embraced briefly in the shrubbery, and returned to the garden to find the crowd rapidly thinning out. Shirley and Gerald Stanton were standing on the gravel sweep in front of the house, expediting departures with pleasant remarks and an occasional handshake. As Belinda and Adrian came up, Mrs. Walston broke off from an ecstatic commentary.

"And here's Miss Plowman, too-oo," she trilled. "Such a lovely family party! And what a privilege for us all to have a peep at these wonderful grounds. As I was saying, if only Mavis could have been here, but the dear, good girl's helping those poor disabled folk down at St. Christopher's Home this week. At least, I *hope* she's being a good girl," Mrs. Walston added, with an arch glance at Gerald Stanton. "Superintendent Thomas sent Constable Bly round just before I left home, to ask where she was. He thought she had some information he wanted."

Once again, there was a fractional pause.

"Yet another motor accident that they want witnesses of, I expect," Gerald Stanton said. "There seems no end to them. So good of you to come this afternoon, Mrs. Walston. . . . If you'll excuse me, I must just have a word with one or two other people."

Shirley Stanton gave her niece a quick meaning look.

"I insist on sending you home in a taxi, Mrs. Walston," she said. "It was splendid of you to toil out here on this hot afternoon. Belinda, dear, just run in and ring Bright's, will you? Ask them to send one up at once."

Smothering a grin at her aunt's disengagement tactics, Belinda ran into the house and across the hall to the telephone room. Numbers frequently used were posted up, and she lifted the receiver preparatory to dialling. She realized immediately that the extension was in use, and in the same instant recognized her uncle's voice.

"St. Christopher's?" she heard. "This is the Corbury police station calling. We have an urgent message for one of your helpers, Miss Mavis Fletcher. Right? Her aunt, Mrs. Walston, has been knocked down by a car and is seriously hurt. Miss Fletcher should come to Corbury at once. We are sending a car for her. Will you break the news to her, and see that she's ready? Thank you."

There was a click, and a silence. Belinda stood paralysed in body and mind. A door banged at the back of the house. Suddenly galvanized into action she dashed out, almost into Adrian's arms.

"I don't understand what's happening," she gasped. "Come in here."

She dragged him into the deserted drawing room, and steadying herself with a supreme effort, repeated the conversation which she had just overheard.

"Adrian, what can it mean?" she implored.

"I don't know." He looked grim. "Whatever it means, it's got to be stopped. We must ring this place."

They crammed into the telephone room, and he searched the directory frantically, while Belinda looked up the Fairport code. He dialled, and after what seemed an eternity they heard the ringing tone. It stopped.

"St. Christopher's, Fairport. Superintendent Pollard speaking," came a voice.

Adrian gave an audible gasp of astonishment.

"Belinda Plowman and Beresford here, sir," he half-stuttered. "Somebody's sent a hoax message to Miss Mavis Fletcher saying her aunt's had an accident. She hasn't. She's here—Edgehill Court—and perfectly all right. A car may come to fetch her—Miss Fletcher, I mean."

"Thanks very much, Mr. Beresford," Pollard replied. "Sensible of you both to ring promptly. As I happen to be here, having a chat with her, I'll see she isn't bothered. Good-bye."

He rang off. They stood speechless, staring at each other. At the other end, Pollard smiled and resolved that the engaging pair should never know that he had just checked the call with Corbury police station before they rang.

Outside her office, the brisk grey-haired matron hovered anxiously.

"It was a hoax, Miss Goodbody," he told her. "I'm so glad you called me out of the room before giving Miss Fletcher the message. Now I'll just finish my talk with her, and then wait, if I may, as I think the hoaxer may turn up. If he does, just show him in to us, and keep her out of the way, will you?"

"Indeed I will," Miss Goodbody replied indignantly. "The wickedness of it! I only hope he'll be punished."

Pollard returned to the sitting room where Toye and Superintendent Hart of Allchester were manfully keeping up a general conversation.

"So sorry for the interruption, Miss Fletcher," he said as he sat down. "I was just saying, wasn't I, that we're very interested in any strangers about in Corbury at the beginning of last December, and that it's in connection with Bernard

Lister's death? Do you by any chance remember anybody making a pretext to call at Stanton and Mundy's?"

Mavis Fletcher's pleasant, rather homely face registered intense concentration. Nice girl, Pollard thought, taking in her mass-produced summer frock and unimaginative hair style. Not over intelligent, but dependable. He wondered what desperate step to silence her Gerald Stanton, now presumably speeding towards Fairport, had in mind.

"Yes, I do!" she suddenly exclaimed in a triumphant tone. "It was a Friday afternoon, and Mr. Stanton wanted to get off early. I couldn't get the man to make an appointment for the week after, so Mr. Stanton saw him, but told me to come in and remind him about a Council meeting in ten minutes. There wasn't one really, of course, but it worked."

By dint of further questions Pollard established the date as Friday, 1 December, and went on to the caller's appearance.

"He was pale, and wore dark glasses. I remember thinking it was funny, right in the middle of winter. He had an overcoat, and hat and scarf, and was rather short."

"It must be fine to have an observant secretary like you," Pollard told her encouragingly. "We can hardly expect you to remember his name, I suppose?"

"I can, as a matter of fact," Mavis Fletcher said, blushing at his compliment. "I made a note of it, in case there was to be an account. It was Spinner. Mr. Spinner."

Toye involuntarily shifted his position.

"You've been most helpful, Miss Fletcher," Pollard said. "Now I expect you're anxious to be back on the job in this busy place, so we won't hold you up any longer."

He got up to open the door for her, and she departed, still blushing.

"This clinches it," he said, looking at his watch. "It's not an open and shut case even now, but I'm pulling him in. He ought to turn up in about ten minutes—unless he thinks better of it."

It was a tense and apparently interminable wait. When at last footsteps and voices approached, Toye moved quietly to a position behind the door. It opened and Gerald Stanton was shown into the room, an expression of anxious solicitude on his face. It froze. Before he could speak Pollard had stepped forward.

"Gerald Stanton," he said, "I charge you with the murder of Bernard Lister on the fourteenth of December last—"

It took all three of them to overpower him, and get him to the car.

On arrival at Stanton and Mundy's office some time later, Pollard was admitted by Toye, who informed him that Mr. Mundy was raring to get off to Allchester to fix legal representation for Mr. Stanton.

"Seems a decent young chap," he added. "The arrest's knocked him for six."

Pollard decided on a sympathetic but brisk line.

"I quite appreciate that you want to make legal arrangements for your partner," he said, "but there are certain points I want clarified. You realize, presumably, that Sir Miles LeWarne's will was officially drawn up by Stanton and Mundy. Both partners are named as executors. I want a statement of the part you yourself took in the matter."

An expression of bewilderment and slight alarm appeared in John Mundy's face.

"As a matter of fact," he said, "I'm prepared to state on oath that I had no hand whatever in drafting the will. Sir Miles was an old friend of the Plowmans, and Gerald Stanton always handled his business. Lately, if anything wanted doing, he'd be rung up and asked to go over to Edgehill Court, to spare Sir Miles coming in."

"Didn't it strike you as unusual that absolutely nothing in connection with the will was dealt with in this office in the first instance?" Pollard asked.

"Not under the circumstances. Everyone knew Sir Miles was bowled over by Roger LeWarne's death, and would have to rethink what he was going to do about his estate. Gerald Stanton said that he was frightfully steamed up, and had a thing about the new will leaking out, and that he, Gerald, had undertaken to handle the whole business himself, including the typing. It so happened that Mrs. Stanton was away, so he worked on the thing at home in the evenings. All the office did was to provide a couple of chaps to go over and witness the signature. It was all perfectly reasonable. Gerald Stanton never wanted to act in the matter—quite understandably in view of his wife's expectations—but Sir Miles was insistent and in view of the long family link and the old man's distressed state, he gave in. . . . Isn't it time you stated categorically just what you are driving at? I am, after all, a partner in this firm."

Mr. Engle leant across the table and handed a letter to Pollard.

"This appears to be relevant to Mr. Mundy's last statement," he said.

Pollard read it. It was a brief, straightforward statement of Gerald Stanton's reluctance to draw up Sir Miles LeWarne's will, in view of his wife's being the chief beneficiary, but concluding with his undertaking to do so because of the very special circumstances.

Feeling inexplicably that something was wrong, Pollard read it again with close attention to detail. It was typed on the firm's official stationery, headed Stanton and Mundy, Solicitors, 100 High Street, Corbury AL3 OT2. The date was 7 December 1971. He stared and stared. Then, in a flash of illumination, he was in Superintendent Thomas's room on the occasion of his first visit. . . .

A few minutes later he returned from putting through a call in an adjoining room, and saw Toye look at him sharply. He picked up the letter. Three faces were turned towards him.

"This letter," he said quietly, "was not written on 7 December 1971, for the simple reason that the Allchester area was not allotted its postcodes until the beginning of November, 1972. Whoever wrote the letter overlooked this fact, and obviously put it among Sir Miles LeWarne's papers with intent to mislead. I imagine that what I am driving at must now be clear to you, Mr. Mundy."

White and tense, John Mundy asked if he should go to Edgehill Court, and break the news of her husband's arrest to Mrs. Stanton.

"I would rather go myself," Pollard said. "You can rely on me to treat her with consideration. I suggest that you go direct to Allchester, and see Mr. Stanton."

As the door closed, Mr. Engle remarked that the prosecution would have the whale of a time putting its case together.

"Is the wife involved too?" he asked, gathering papers together.

"My hunch is, not," Pollard replied. "It's important to establish if she really was away from Corbury during that last week of LeWarne's life. If so, I can't quite see Stanton discussing it with her over the phone or putting his scheme on paper."

After further discussion of immediate steps to be taken he left for Edgehill Court, feeling excited and triumphant. This feeling, he knew, would pass, leaving distaste for the outcome of the case and at best emotionless satisfaction at a job carried through. But at this moment there was the exhilarating sense of achievement against apparently impossible odds.

At the beginning of Edge Crescent he slowed down to pass a stationary car, and as he did so Belinda Plowman and Adrian Beresford scrambled out of it. Taut and breathless, Belinda asked if he were going to her house.

"I am," Pollard said, "but not for the reason that has been worrying you. But there's no joy for you all, I'm afraid. Mr. Stanton has been charged with Bernard Lister's murder."

"Uncle Gerald!" she gasped incredulously.

"See what you can do for them, Beresford. I suggest that you both keep clear for a few minutes while I call on Mr. Plowman."

"I'll do that thing, sir," Adrian replied gravely.

Looking back as he rang the bell, Pollard saw the pair clasped in a prolonged embrace. One happy outcome, perhaps, he thought.

Mark Plowman opened the door, stood stiffly and braced himself.

"I'm afraid I've come with bad news," Pollard said, and went on to deliver it. He watched the chain reactions reflected in Mark Plowman's eyes: unbelief—stupefaction—relief—horror—perplexity.

"I'm going over to tell Mrs. Stanton now," he said. "I suggest you and Mrs. Plowman stand by: she might be glad to spend the night here."

"Yes, of course. Anything we can do, naturally . . . perhaps you'd ring me from there. . . ." Bewildered and uncertain, Mark Plowman tried to orientate himself. "One doesn't want to butt in. . . . My God, I just can't take it in. Surely there must be a mistake somewhere? I mean, Gerald . . ."

Interesting, Pollard thought, as he drove on, how in this hour of crisis, Plowman's basic lack of confidence came uppermost. All that blasting about was a defence mechanism, of course.

In the just-failing light Edgehill Court had a dreamlike beauty, he thought. He drew up, and in the same moment

Shirley Stanton emerged looking both angry and worried. She registered blank astonishment, then quickly took herself in hand.

"Superintendent Pollard? But what a surprise! Have you run across my husband by any chance? He went off hours ago and I'm really getting quite anxious about him."

"May I come in, Mrs. Stanton?" Pollard asked.

At his tone she gave him a startled look, and led the way into the drawing room.

"Please tell me why you are here," she said, with habitual directness. "Surely Scotland Yard isn't concerned with motor accidents?"

He repeated his formula about being the bringer of bad news.

"I regret to have to tell you that your husband has been charged with the murder of your cousin, Bernard Lister. He has been taken to Allchester, and will appear before a magistrates' court tomorrow."

Shirley Stanton stared at him, speechless, and he watched her struggle to regain her habitual composure. For a moment he wondered if she could succeed.

"I've never heard anything so preposterous," she said at last. "It's sheer lunacy. They hadn't even met for over twenty years. . . . Whoever is responsible for this outrageous mistake is going to regret it, I can promise you."

"We have evidence," Pollard told her, "that Bernard Lister visited your husband at his office on 1 December last year."

She's intelligent, he thought, watching her assimilate this information and seize on its implications.

"What on earth do you mean?" Shirley Stanton demanded. "Are you saying that Bernard was blackmailing my husband?"

The telephone bell cut in before he could reply. With an expression of utter exasperation she turned and went swiftly out of the room. Standing in the doorway Pollard tried to listen in, but without success.

When she returned he was startled by her expression. She stood for a few minutes in silence, supporting herself by resting her hands on the back of the chair.

"That was John Mundy," she said at last. "He says Gerald has admitted to having forged Sir Miles's will. This place isn't mine after all. . . . Gerald has stated on oath that I didn't know. . . ."

Her voice trailed off, and she stared unseeingly across the room.

"You will understand," Pollard said, deliberately matter-of-fact, "that there are some questions I must ask you."

She appeared to revert to her normal composed self, and suggested that they should sit down.

"Thank you," Pollard said. "My first question is this. Are you prepared to state on oath that you did not know that the will purporting to be Sir Miles LeWarne's, and which was granted probate, was, in fact, a forgery?"

Shirley Stanton looked at him as if pitying his lack of understanding.

"I am," she replied, without comment.

"Secondly," Pollard pursued, "where were you during the week of 5 December to 12 December last year."

"That is easily verifiable, you will find. From the fifth to the ninth I was in London, as one of the organizers of the Interior Décor in the Seventies Exhibition. From the ninth to the twelfth I was staying at Medstead School, with Mr. and Mrs. Craig. He is a housemaster there."

"Thank you." Pollard put away his notebook. "Mr. Mundy will have told you that he is making arrangements for Mr. Stanton's legal representation. He will, I am sure, be in constant touch with you. Meanwhile, I suggest that you allow me to ring your brother and sister-in-law, and ask them to come over."

He thought that she smiled faintly, as if he were being naïve.

"Not just at the moment, thank you," she said. "I want to be alone for a bit, to straighten things out in my mind, if possible. You've been very kind: I appreciate it."

She rose with dignity. After fractional hesitation Pollard rose too and followed her to the front door.

His head seemed hardly to have touched the pillow when the persistent bleeping of the bedside telephone dragged him up into early daylight.

"Thomas here," a harassed voice said. "Sorry to tell you there's been a disaster: Mrs. Stanton's made away with herself. Took her car out some time during the night, and drove it over the edge of a chalk pit. Farm labourer spotted the wreckage on his way to work. . . ."

When he had rung off Pollard got up and went to the next room to rouse Toye, who opened the door at once.

"I heard your blower going," he said, as Pollard took up a stance with his back to the window, and began to talk.

Toye sat on the edge of the bed and listened, impeccable even at this hour in neat striped pyjamas and his horn-rims.

"You couldn't have prevented it, sir," he said. "You'd no grounds for posting a chap outside, let alone in the house. Doesn't it look as though she was in with her husband after all?"

"I don't believe it," Pollard said emphatically. "He killed her, you know, by destroying for ever the image of herself she'd built up and identified with."

Toye considered.

"You could say Lister did, by putting the screw on Stanton. He hated her enough to do her. Remember what he wrote on those cuttings from the *Courier*?"

"Quite true," Pollard agreed, looking at Toye with some surprise. "Why was he so bloody-minded? The old Plowmans and his maternal grandparents were partly responsible, I suppose."

"Not to mention those chaps who cooked the Corbury Charters, and brought Lister down to these parts to dig it all up," Toye said meditatively. "Buried in the past, how it all began, isn't it?"

# *Epilogue*

The *Corbury Courier*, first published in 1830 during the town's death throes as a Rotten Borough, kept its readers abreast of the traumatic events in their midst by means of a special edition reporting Gerald Stanton's arrest and his wife's suicide, and generous enlargement of subsequent weekly issues. Winnie Rudd complained that with the paper such a size you couldn't find your way about in the thing, and concentrated on the pictures.

"Them giving out the funeral was strictly private didn't stop folk sending a heap of flowers for the poor soul," she commented, looking at a photograph of Shirley Stanton's grave. "Though there'll always be some as says she was in with her husband over the will, for all that he's sworn on his bible oath that she wasn't."

She turned over a page and subjected Superintendent Pollard's countenance to close scrutiny.

"Don't look a bad sort, that Scotland Yard detective," she pronounced. "Here, take the blessed paper. I can't wade through any more of it."

Horace Rudd lit his pipe, and settled down for a good read. He was deep in the report of Gerald Stanton's committal to the Crown Court on a homicide charge when his wife asked him when he thought Corbury people would be getting their rights.

"It'll be nice taking a turn in the grounds up to Edgehill Court on a fine Sunday afternoon," she said. "I've always thought I'd like to look inside the place, too."

Horace gave it as his opinion that anything to do with the law always took a month of Sundays. He ploughed on steadily, taking the pages in their numerical sequence until he arrived at the editorial. It carried the puzzling title PREPOSTER

OUS PEDANTRY, and he fetched the dictionary, a leftover from his son's schooldays.

"PEDANT, one who overrates or parades book learning," he read, and not much enlightened, embarked on the article.

"Did you ever hear the like?" he exclaimed indignantly a few minutes later. "There's some chap called Catchpole over to Allchester saying King Edgar never gave us no charter, and what we've got's a fake, and we've no right to the Millenary."

Winnie snorted.

"That lot over there 'ud say anything but their prayers."

"He's saying," Horace pursued, "that Corbury copied the Allchester charter, and it's proved because he wrote in Skinner instead of Spinner, same as they did, for some chap's name."

"Lot o' rubbish! I never could do with history at school. Now geography's different. You can go and see for yourself if Australia's there, but who's to know what went on hundreds of years back with all the people dead and gone? Tell me that."

Horace hesitated, dimly aware that the Roman coin he had found at the dig was relevant to the argument, but finding himself unequal to presenting his case convincingly.

"Seen the advert asking someone to lend one o' those brindled bull terriers to be St. Gundryth's dog in the pageant?" his wife enquired.

"This Catchpole says there never was such a person as St. Gundryth."

"Well, there's the parish church named after her, isn't there? That chap's got a surprise waiting for him one day," Winnie added cryptically.

Horace read the article a second time with knitted brow. Then he fetched writing materials and began a letter to the Editor of the *Corbury Courier*.

Dear Sir, [he wrote]

Once again I take up my pen to support your paper's stand on King Edgar's charter and the Millenary a matter of weeks away. . . .

## ABOUT THE AUTHOR

ELIZABETH LEMARCHAND was born in Barnstaple in Devon and was educated at a convent school. She took a degree in history and geography at University College, Exeter, and then spent thirty-two years in the teaching profession. Now a retired headmistress, she has made a most successful second career as a writer of mystery novels and two short stories.

# "THE BEST POPULAR NOVEL TO BE PUBLISHED IN AMERICA SINCE *THE GODFATHER.*"

—Stephen King

# RED DRAGON

## by Thomas Harris, author of BLACK SUNDAY

If you never thought a book could make you quake with fear, prepare yourself for RED DRAGON. For in its pages, you will meet a human monster, a tortured being driven by a force he cannot contain, who pleasures in viciously murdering happy families. When you discover how he chooses his victims, you will never feel safe again.

Buy this book at your local bookstore or use this handy coupon for ordering:

Inside Boston Doctor's Hospital, patients are dying.
No one knows why,
No one but . . .

# THE SISTERHOOD

Nurses bound together in mercy. Pledged to end human suffering. Sworn to absolute secrecy. But, within the Sisterhood, evil blooms. Under the white glare of the operating room, patients survive the surgeon's knife. Then, in the dark hollow silence of the nighttime hospital, they die. Suddenly, inexplicably, horribly. No one knows why. No one but the Sisterhood.

One man, a tough, bright doctor, risks his career, his very life, to unmask the terrifying mystery. One woman, a beautiful and dedicated young nurse, unknowingly holds the answer. Together they will discover that no one is safe from . . .

# THE SISTERHOOD

### A Novel by
### MICHAEL PALMER

"Compassion turns to terror . . . Riveting reading, I couldn't put it down."

—V. C. Andrews, author of *Flowers in the Attic*